FIVE
LOST YEARS
by Christina Alexandra

Foreword by John Paul Brady, M.D.

FIVE LOST YEARS

by Christina Alexandra

Scripture quotations taken from the
HOLY BIBLE, NEW INTERNATIONAL VERSION
Copyright 1973, 1978, 1984, International Bible Society

Dry Bones Press
P. O. Box 597
Roseville, CA 95678–0597

http://www.drybones.com/

(415) 707–2129

Publisher's Cataloging–in–Publication

Alexandra, Christina—
    Five Lost Years / by Christina Alexander
    p.   cm.
    ISBN 1–883938–46–5
1. Schizophrenia. 2. Psychology—Patients. 3. Patient response.
4. Christianity—Fundamentalist/"Born Again" 5. Healing
I. Title. II. Author.

Dedication

To Mum and "Joy," who stayed close by my side, all through my illness—and filled my world with love.

To dear Dr. John Paul Brady, What can I say. A wonderful saint, and the most humanitarian person I have ever known. Thank you eternally for saving my life, and, leading me to receive Jesus Christ as my personal Savior. That says it all.

Dear Jesus Christ—I love you forever. Your salvation is the best thing that has ever happened to me!

Forward

Schizophrenia is a mental illness that afflicts about one percent of the population. Like diabetes and gout, it tends to run in families although in many cases there is no family history of the disorder. Typically symptoms first have their onset while the patient is in his/her late teens or early 20s. The disorder is characterized by disturbances in multiple psychological processes, including those involved in thinking, emotional reactions, and the motivation of behavior. Thus in any given patient one might see odd or bizarre ideation, the presence of hallucinations or delusions, inappropriate emotional responses, social isolation or withdrawal and the failure to develop adequate social and interpersonal skills. When full-blown the disorder can have a devastating effect on the patients adjustment. Fortunately, some patients only have a single major episode and largely recover from the illness. Others have multiple episodes, perhaps separated by months or even years before showing sustained improvement. Finally some continue to have severe episodes and never maintain an adequate adjustment in their relationships with others, their capacity to be gainfully employed and their functioning in other important life areas.

Although schizophrenia has been recognized in one form or another since antiquity, it is only in the last decade or so that psychiatrists and behavioral scientists have appreciated its nature. There still tends to be misunderstanding and many myths about schizophrenia in the population at large; some of these are still held by persons in the medical and allied medical professions. It may be helpful to mention several of these.

One myth, common as recently as a decade ago, was that schizophrenia was the result of social factors. One crude form of this was that when societal pressures are too great, or society changes too rapidly, some individuals develop schizophrenia. Of course there have always been great societal pressures. Only their nature has changed over the millennia. The view that society is changing too rapidly has been the case throughout history; each generation feels that those which preceded it were periods of more gentle or more gradual change than the one in which it is currently living. In addition, there is simply no scientific evidence that the rate of social change, societal pressures, or societal problems such as poverty or high crime rate increase the frequency of schizophrenia.

A related myth is that schizophrenia is caused by poor child rearing practices. The simplistic notion that schizophrenia is caused by poor mothering led to the presumptive term "schizophren=ogenic mother" some years ago. As has often been the case in the history of psychiatry, psychiatrists and other observers mistakenly took the consequences of a major mental disorder for its causes. The stress produced in the family with a schizophrenia teenager or young adult is often so great that other family members show varying degrees of disturbance, defensiveness, etc. When such behaviors were observed in mothers or other family members, they are usually a result of living with a person with schizophrenia. In any case there is no scientific evidence that schizophrenia is the result of some feature of the parent-child relationship or to other family influences. This is not to say that once a person develops schizophrenia, the quality of the person's adjustment and the course of the illness may not be influenced to some extent by the quality of family relationships. Of course this is the case with chronic medical illnesses in general; for example the course of chronic and poorly controlled diabetes in a young person or the course of dementia in an elderly person.

Another myth popular some 20 years ago was that schizophrenia is not a disease but society's label of a person who revolts against the poor values of the culture in which he lives. A highly romanticized version of this was popularized by the Scottish poet R.D. Lang. This view claimed that the person labeled with schizophrenia is simply adjusting as best he/she can to a crazy world. It was even implied that schizophrenia is a desirable or rewarding condition to have. The notion that schizophrenia is in some way enjoyable is nonsense. One need only ask patients afflicted with this devastating disorder to describe their frightening experiences while acutely psychotic, and the often continuing effects of the illness on their quality of adjustment, for long periods of time, to see the absurdity of this idea. Schizophrenia is no more enjoyable than gout or tuberculosis.

Another myth is that persons with schizophrenia are dangerous or unpredictable. In fact there was no evidence that patients with this medical illness are any more dangerous than "normal" people. Much of this myth is attributable to the excessive publicity given to persons who commit major crimes who have a history of mental illness. The point is, that the percentage of persons with mental illness that commit major crimes is less than the percentage of the general population that is responsible for similar criminal deeds. This misconception is made worse by fictional accounts of persons with schizophrenia committing murder and other crimes.

A final myth is that schizophrenia cannot be helped by medical treatment. Although there is much 'room for further progress, important developments have occurred in the treatment and management of this major medical illness. Flare ups of the acute symptoms (psychosis) can be controlled and prevented in the majority of patients with the aid of newly developed medications. The overall adjustment of the patient with schizophrenia can be greatly assisted by planful and knowledgeable counseling by a psychiatrist, clinical psychologist or other health-care professional trained specifically to treat this disorder. There are exciting recent developments in understanding the chemistry of the brain and the organization of the central nervous system which may lead to additional progress in the treatment and management of this condition.

This book is the personal account of a young woman afflicted with schizophrenia. She does not conform to any of the stereotypes often held about persons with this condition. The author is a highly intelligent woman who is intuitive in interpersonal relationships and has never been dangerous or destructive in any way. As the reader will learn from these pages she has had several incapacitating episodes of acute psychosis which greatly altered the direction of her life and her capacity to work and to love. She is now recovering from the disorder and has been free of the major symptoms of schizophrenia for almost two years. The author is now rediscovering many of her creative gifts, including writing and painting, developing trusting and loving relationships with other persons and making progress, albeit slowly, toward a better quality of life and being an active contributor to the community.

One can learn much from reading textbook accounts of schizophrenia and new developments in its understanding and treatment in the medical literature. However, one can gain a different and vital perspective of the nature of the disorder by reading an insightful account of the illness by one who has experienced it. This autobiographical narrative provides such an understanding.

John Paul Brady, M.D.
Kenneth E. Appel Professor of Psychiatry,
University of Pennsylvania

A One Act Play

Parallel an image I remain
A symmetric shape in an ingress
Absorbed within a compliant plane
A mere face. Encompassed in flesh
Now lucid lambrequins fragment
While muffled voices murmur
Like some ethereal tribal chant
As they blend together—one resonant
An—undiscerning spotlight reveals all
While I stand circumscribed in a white drop of light
To them a mere novel entity they saw
A recherche' spectacle of wheel—a sight!
But soon the array must terminate
the curtains hail to a conclusion
And as the assemblage must dissipate
I am left suffused in despondent disillusion
I thank you for your easeful presence
For a cordial individual in a crowd
Who came to the show to be a friend
Rather than view an enigma then go.

Man

Why must you waste
and rot
infinitely.
Trying to delve past
your morbid friends
and unfetter
yourself—
from brustied shackles
soon you shall see
that I too
cannot bear their torn
faces
fluid expressions
affected graces
languid and lost
you express more then five
dimensions of glass
while I equally
playfully call your losses
you press to accentuate
the morbidity of a single
thought
you spool, to drill the
relevance of your superioritic
intricacies.
You whine and the faces of
your enemies.
Rearing endlessly into
your channels
you chafe as you—reel,
and bind your incessant
anarchism.
While man sees his
face contorted from device,
looks at his hand
and realizes his grace.

She

She dies ever so frightful
white lily hands frozen
to the stilled earthen dusk
stilled on toes of silence
peeking heavenly into her
haven of secrecy
blemished walnut and smoked iris
she waits patronly to be told
the mist still clears
outside her window
the snow must fall
and cover over and under
all she does; but know.

You and I

Patterned footsteps
ruin the purple mist of my
brain
we sleep—soundly
ignore all else
is clamor
blue veiled moments spin
eternities on our mind.
And we wait
for beauty to behold justice.
Degraveled times wait
sentinels still the duration
your orbs touch mine
blue cobalt branches
will shatter all else
I could protest.

My Fair Maiden

She had eyes of gleaming gold
my fair maiden
she let me touch her
pursue and hold
my fair maiden
crossed the lashes from my right
and ripped me—clean out of sight
now I wander
glen and dale
as the slow moon sinks aglow
and I tiptoe hind her
skin and pale
with her bosom burning bright
and I see her slip in
barns, and sleep conscious
with the night.
But the cold death of the
slaughter house—keeps her up
all the night
now I wish she would
come home to me—and tell me of
her joy—that she met
in Scotland's heather lands
a ruddy—summer's boy
but her pigtails no longer trapped
and she screams for father now
as I grow old, weak and weary
wishing her to hold.

Bloodied Warrior

Bloodied warrior
bows to his niece
hatchet in hand
his purple beads gleam
the fading suns
beaten horizons
of Earthly musk.
Stiff—he's electrified
and feels his tautness
from knee to sunken
stone.
While his fingers
grasp the velvetness of
his preys internal organs.
he dances only
for the gods.
Though Job takes
his cut, only to spill
mortals entrails onto the
bloodied plane.

Moth

I found her seeped in yonder grove
her melton wings, her filigreed bow
the poor moth, was spotted still
so I made her a bed—in my
window sill.
I protected her from might and foe
and searched the heavens
for her name.
Though I met her only once in
proof
I danced with her
it was my youth.

Cavaliers Death

Upon wayward rocks we
stray
to meet and kiss the
kindred souls. Their tiny faces—
bent to lite, kiss the day.
Shivers send their ripples
to confusion.
To scratch the steeple blue.
Cavaliers death.

Chapter One

At a young age of 14, life is of a complicated sort. Life at home is becoming worse and worse. The unpleasant feelings undulating over and over again. I feel as if I am the puzzle piece to the wrong picture. I don't seem to have any friends at school. I am the shyest in my clubs. My life feels like a pin cushion with all the needles being placed in the tenderest parts. I have lost all sense of identity. My mind becoming a fortress; the walls are so great. I find I don't speak the same language as everybody else. I never smile. In school I am a loner but for one friend. The hobbies my art and music now entrap me like a fish on a line. There is no new insight, no way to save myself, from misfortune and misery.

Today I have an appointment with a new doctor. I am welcomed into his plush office and the secretary asks me to sit down. The place somehow looking like a womb, yet with the casualness of colors, sends the place in poor taste and bad rhythm. My eyes gaze over the magazines—yet my interest in bettering myself seems trivial.

I am seated in the doctors office, he is a tall, handsome dark-haired man. We adjust ourselves in our chairs. I can tell from one, that he has no interest in me. We speak for quite some time. I tell him how ugly I am, how I have no intelligence and how I don't fit in with people. He gives me a taut smile and suggests that I take sleeping pills and that I am only going through a stormy adolescence. I leave with the same deep depression I came in with.

Chapter Two

The loud buzz of the alarm hastens me out of a wakeful slumber. I rub my eyes and glance first upon the walls of my refuge. This, a peaceful scrap of morning—when everyone else is asleep, is a land I dream of and have learned to cherish over the years. I step slowly onto the cold floorboards and stumble my way across the room to shut the windows. As I gaze at the hazy image in the mirror, I realize that I am not beautiful, let alone—pretty, but down right ugly with this stark white skin. I set my morning ritual out—first the foundation (a muddied concoction) I smooth on with the uncaring attitude which comes to one only with years upon years of the stagnant routine. I dabble on blush, smearing it onto my cheeks and then eye shadow, mascara, eyebrow pencil and lastly, lipstick.

My wardrobe is carefully selected from indecision upon indecision. I grab my books and eat a hasty meal. Outside, a light snow is falling, and I walk determinedly to school. This is the part of the day I enjoy most, I lose myself in fantasy where I am queen and nature this white wonderland—my world. The crystalized trees, the various sentinels protecting me. Even though my family may say I'll never have any friends. I know that at school I do. I have made it my goal, for the past two years, to be as popular as possible—honor society, A.R.T.W., dancer in the senior plays, marching band and concert band. Coming out of my shy years these are more turbulent years. My superficiality is like a rock.

As I enter the heavy metal front door of school, a couple of boys approach me and one more. I can see, feel, as I josh with each of the boys that the girls in the cafeteria are glancing over at me and talking about me, wearing sour expressions. A deliberate sort of move. The buzzer rings which announces to us to go to our home rooms. As I get swept in the tide, I find my one and only girlfriend. We exchange quick hellos. We are not really friends, but all, I have except for the entourage I have gained. I doodle my way through most of the day and as 3:00 draws near—I feel the same wave of panic that I feel every day when school ends and I must go home.

I begrudgingly travel through the icy drifts of snow on the one mile long trek to my home. I am greeted at the door with an angry face. An argument as usual. Who's right and who's wrong, we barely know ourselves. I run screaming up to my room I feel this imbalance she loves me, she hates me. I slam the door and put on one of my reclusive tapes: Genesis, and light up the joint I have saved. Somehow all problems seem to dissipate into the starry evening as I sit staring out the window. My family bangs on the door. I reflect—its been this way for two years now. I hate school (the people talking about me) and I detest my home life. Sherman, Sherman, Sherman why won't you save me from this? I press my cold trembling hands to my face as my body wracks with sobs that will lull me to sleep.

The next morning I plead with my mother, "please let me change schools". "Everybody is talking about me and I can't defend myself." A look, on the bright edge of understanding startles me. "Yes Christina we will look into some other schools."

Chapter Three

Living at home is becoming an arduous task. No longer do I feel like a part of the family. For some indiscernible reason, my sisters and brothers, my mother in particular, are becoming unknown, estranged... Every movement I make is no longer in sync with or in concurrence with their desires. There are verbal shouting matches all too often. I feel a nausea creeping up my throat as I try to become what I am supposed to be whatever that may be. I act out all too often, feel myself saying strange things that make a common sense to me but are so bitter to my kin. I suppose my lack of a social life—the steady deterioration and disintegration of self grinds on their nerves. I am the "sick" one, the oddball. My speech sings to me but is merely a nuisance to those closest to me. I can't please anyone. I don't feel "right".

Having dinner with my family, the voices seem inordinately loud. Crashing—pulling me into an abysmal hole. There is no escape from this pit. I see the contorted faces of the family council staring at me seething—wild eyes, a circle around me as the faces get larger and larger, beckoning me to agree with what I don't understand. Their language shouts at me with cryptic desire. Obviously all love is gone. It has been replaced by a deep hatred. The family mystic rites and mystic rituals—me the sacrifice. I try to defend myself, but there is no longer anyone there to move for me. The moment has gone and their words have now shattered any hope or desire I have to live. I flee. Up the stairs and into my own private heaven. My room—where all is ordinary and understandable. My room; my possessions stare at me and something tells me it's time. There is no longer anything left. I crawl into bed. The conversation beats on my brain with incessance, curiosity and malice. All of a sudden, I am in the bathroom. One sleeping pill... Two, and the rest have disappeared. I don't care. Somewhere deep in my mind, I realize I could surely end up a vegetable. But this one thing no longer matters or has essence. Back in my bedroom I stare out my window—glow pink electric blue as I watch the trees in the night breeze, somehow I feel at one with them. I sit. I stare. I long to leave my body. Soon I have entered another world. Peace. I can no longer find myself. Where has everything gone? Sleep. Then, the noise—a harsh raucous croak. "Telephone Christina." I slide one leg over the edge of the bed. Where the hell am I? What has happened? I took some pills. That's right oh, the phone. I have to get the, PHONE! The phone, the most important. My mother calls to me. I can't walk. Everything has retarded slow motion—no, I am not walking—I am actually floating—where am I going? My mother's face stares at me. Angry. "What have you done— what have you done!" I don't know. What the hell have you done. Her face is a twisted shell, carved in wood, a totem pole. She towers above me then vanishes. I am alone—I have to get the phone. Actually this is all very amusing. I have the smile of a broken puppet pasted on my face. Hah! I took a bottle of, er no—I drank something? The stairs are looming in front of me, a great precipice. Suddenly I am walking across the living room just like an old Hanes pantyhose commercial. My feet are no longer in contact with the ground. Hey, this is neat. I am walk- ing—but no, it feels more like stumbling four feet above the ground. I cannot coordinate my movements. As I look down, my feet merely dan- gle. All around me takes on a kaleidoscopic hue. Like looking into a Christmas bulb, the images are so comical. There's my sister. The voice of a dictator. "Here—you sit here." She points to the seat in the tiny, dark, undecorated bathroom downstairs and then she's gone. I wait and my body feels for as to stay in one place. My God, I can't move! Hours pass. I wait in the room with one small window. There's just one ques- tion I have. Why isn't anybody helping me? Shouldn't I be. In the... Hospital? Oh, I feel nauseous. I want to vomit, but how—can I? Where is my mother? I must get upstairs. They're gone. Panic envelopes me... Somehow after hours of described movements, I make it up the stairs. But I don't remember going. up them! There are my mother and sister ensconced on her bed reading the P.D.R. What have I just said? I scream "Why aren't we at... the... hospital?" as merely a slur. I am pla- cated—the voice of a child. "We don't know what you took darling." "But I showed you the empty bottle." The ride from house to infirmary is lost in neglect.

At last, I feel the cool, white sterility of hospital sheets smooth against my body. But where are my clothes? Somebody took them. Oh, I have to go to the bathroom. But this damn robe, what is it? It clings to me, yet it is exposing my full back view. I desperately clutch at it. I have to go to the bathroom, here, help me out of bed! The figures—sad faces stand staring around me. Mum, please don't look so sad! There it is—a potty. I crouch down—my legs trembling, but somehow this damn robe keeps floating away from the back of my body. I struggle to cover myself. How could anybody see me denuded! This is most embarrassing. I can't go; some time passes into oblivion. There's this man who's sticking something in my arm. Who is he? I struggle—I fight back. One rip and the tube-like snake is torn from the tender bend of my inner arm. My eyes rove, then spot this glass bottle dangling to my left, high above. I don't like it. I have to get rid of it. Just one quick blow of my fist and the i.v. bottle shatters into millions of sharp fragments. But oh, look how pretty they are, lying on the floor—so... pretty! If only, if only I could dance on it. As I feel the pretty crystal pieces beneath my feet. A white figure catches the comer of my eye. Why is this lady in white, the good angel—so horrified! I smile back. They are all struggling with me. I can't move now. My arms and legs are strapped to the bed. Peace—another shot and I am fast asleep, kept in another safe world. Years later, I awake. There is but one sign—a picture in the room—yes, it's a cow; a pretty pink spotted cow, directly in front of me yet miles away its image blurs back, and forth. Hey—I remember that cow, but from where? Oh yes, my childhood. Was it a rhyme, I don't know—but is it really a cow? Now the pastel colors are blending and changing. Where has everyone gone. They are lying on the floor, huddled around me on this plank, like dead animals. Oh—I killed them—no I didn't really kill them, they are sleeping. Relief sweeps over me. I'm in the hospital. Now I know! Someone, please tell them to leave. God. I feel sick. I didn't mean this. I feel so bad. How could I have done this. I try to speak but can't. What did I do, that's the question. As night—a blackness slowly covers over me. So much time passes and I am awake. Again, more sleep as days go by.

I open my eyes slowly and there is but one man in the room, and all has returned to normal. Quiet normalcy. "So Christina, I hear you took some sleeping pills." As flat as death.

I nod in silent ascent. The doctor seems so unconcerned. We exchange a limp handshake. "My name is Dr. Newmark. Can you tell me the similarity between a bike and a bus?"

I can't understand—what is this trim, bald man with the tortoise shell glasses doing here? He doesn't care.

I wait. "They are both modes of transportation." It comes out austere and lacking in life.

We both sit eyeing each other. A confrontation. He steps back.

"I feel you are ok—you should feel better by tomorrow and I will discharge you then", he says.

"But Dr. Newmark—it is N-E-M-A-R-K". I grope for the name. He nods. I stall, I want to ask him why my stomach wasn't pumped.

"I have a skating party to go to Wednesday can you please discharge me soon enough for that?" I feel I am pleading yet my tone will not show that. "You see Sherman Chamberlin is the world to me—second in his class and the only love I have."

A curt smile and Dr. Newmark leaves with a thud of the door. I prop myself up in bed. I have on no makeup, my long dirty blond hair must be showing roots by now, hangs limp—clings to my wet face.

"Hello" A maternal woman in a polyester suit interrupts. She is so abrupt. "You know my son tried suicide." She almost whines, but she is being so pleasant, I like her. She makes me feel good. Her discourse fairly lifts my spirit. She says I am a pretty girl but somehow that seems to be a non-sequitur. Why didn't the doctor tell me if I had lost part of my intelligence? Will it affect me progressively later in life? I feel my eyes wander as she leaves, I drift back to sleep. He doesn't know.

Chapter Four

School life is fine. Honor society for two years or so, marching band, concert band, A.R.T.W. (communications). I have a scholarship to Jenkintown Music School and I am 5th or 6th flute of 24 in school concert band. But something doesn't feel right. My best friend has dropped me, because I am "too popular". My social life is slowly weakening. I work at relationships almost like therapy to compensate for a truly broken home. I defy what my mother says that I will never have any friends. Things don't seem as pleasant as they once were. Somehow the friends that once were, are now demons in disguise. I seem more like an interesting object to them now. A curiosity, something unknown, maybe an enigma. I suppose my priorities are different or maybe just that I am being paranoid. The groups of three and four that used to surround me, have gone. I am no longer one of them, but a foreigner. I run home from school one day and tell my mother in tears, "I've got to find another school". After perusing through brochures we had sent to the house, I go to one of the best private schools in Pennsylvania. The head mistress proclaims, if I received A's and B's at Abington then I could expect C's at Springside. The order is a tall one. As the interview continues, the head mistress, wearing a tweed skirt, proclaims with certain haughtiness, that they will let me know if I am accepted, shortly. Soon I receive a scholarship there.

My first day of school at Springside and the girls all look the same in the plaid uniform. Their mannerisms and aloof self preoccupation seems strained. Most ignore me though my presence is explained in home room. I spend the day going to each class. The academia seems most difficult. After being there several months I am receiving A's and B's but my social life is eradicated. I am the loner it seems, the other girls sensing like animals that I do not come from a background as their own. More and more, again and again, the girls talk about me, in hissing tones behind my back. I tell myself I hate them, to save myself though I long so desperately to be one with them. The teachers like me, especially the art teacher who, because the school year is drawing to an end helped me apply to go to Cornell University to participate in an 'advanced placement program.

Chapter Five

I can't help wondering what it will be like to go to college. I can feel the taste of it sweet on my lips. Imagine yet, an advanced placement program for high school juniors! And I got in!

I fasten my seat belt as the ride begins. My mother and her friend of the rugged breed speak in inexhaustible tones to each other. They speak about me and the intonation becomes a combination of sourness and misgiving. As the car jostles along the road feeling every pothole, I gaze lazily inward to see if there is any verity to this way. Midway into our drive we pass pastures with cows and beast's of the farm. So relaxed. The same stilled conversation. I don't feel a part of the group. I hear them questioning why I should go to Cornell University, if I am bright enough. Yet I am. I'm not supposed to tell, I stifle back the tears. We pull into a nice dining room of a hotel in Ithaca and I am treated to a wonderful steak lunch. The questions seem too probing. I wonder what they feel towards me. I feel I am keeping up with a plastic facade, though I long to break down and really find out what's going on. I don't feel outright hostility, but a subtle disgust. Finally we arrive. The architecture, overwhelming. Huge grey stone buildings. We enter under the archway, I looking up like a child at the fair, the sights are remarkable. My mother comments, "boy, Laura belongs in a place like this". The immediate comparison leaves me cold and uncontained, my every nerve bared on my body. I feel the discomfort developing between us.

After settling me in, the parting is an abrupt one. A slash of kiss on my cheek. The onslaught of tribulation. I feel weak at the knees. I greet my roommate so superficial—and I unpack my bags.

The subjects I have chosen, psychology and conceptual drawing. I go to Noize Center to get my ID card for food, etc. God, how am I going to fair with such brainy people'? Each face seems so strange, like being back in school. I collect myself. The features just a collection of a broken shell yet each one seems too aware of my presence. I make my way up to my room, and lie on my bed. As the evening twilight spreads a blue cover over my bed—spread, soon I am fast asleep.

As morning arrives, I become acutely aware that my roommate and I do not get along. Her divine ways leave no room for imperfection. We decide to take a walk, all seems well at first, but like turning a card over, the shock of the value stands not to argue. I want to get along with her, but she obviously doesn't. Back at the dorm the dictations of my roommate make themselves clear. She also manifests herself with an intelligence unequaled". She likes to submit or relegate me to the role of the "vacant" artist. By this time, I realize I must find a new roommate. I feel so alone. The head proctor of the dorm allows me help. A young girl shares with me her room. Soon enough it seems everybody on the floor dislikes me. What am I doing wrong? However, at lunch, the older students seem to have taken me under their wing. Their questions seem to magnify every part of my soul. I am most thankful though.

Next day after classes, I spend time by myself out on one of the rolling hills of Cornell. Looking over the wide mirage, Ithaca lies before me, stormy eyes, in such sweet form. Her gorges breathing fire only to pelt on the rocks below.

The beauty of the sky and the repetitive green, is the perfect background for my dreaming. I close the book and lie back, the prickly grass against my cheek. Soon, I am awakened out of my reverie. I am approached by one of the male dorm directors. He says there is a party that evening. I don't want to go, but wish not to be rude (I keep mostly to myself). The whole move is making me terribly frightened. We walk back to drop off my book. With him carrying one orange juice and some Vodka we go to the old nearby cemetery dating back to around the 1700's. One can see the day fading fast. A group of 20 or so of us find a nice valley where we each find a velvety patch and curl up there and spend the time smoking and boozing it up. Soon, Matthew and I leave the group and wander into the distorted darkness. We talk, I don't know what about, pass the gorges refulgent in all their glory and all the textured trees bowing to and fro, creaking as they reminisce on earlier days. The summer wind gently washing over us. I know he can tell there is something wrong with me. The night grows ever darker. He seems to be very curious about me rather than having a deep "interest" in me. Knowing of the disillusionment I find myself saying things so that he will actually reject me. We pass a few dorms and there he walks me back to my dorm under a leafy enclosure.

The next morning, a Saturday, two girls and one fellow ask me if I want to go to New York City for the weekend. Ambiguous as the question is, I contemplate. Yes I will go to New York City. I feel pressured although I am thankful these older students have adopted me as their friend. We pack our bags and get in the car. I feel so strange—I hardly know these people. As we have been driving for a half hour or so, Wendy begins to drink some hard liquor. Soon everyone in the car is drinking, including the driver, except me. This frightens me so and they are lighting up joints. Soon we are passing over George Washington Bridge. Horrible images flit through my mind at first, then hold tenure. I immediately search for a seat belt but there are none. My God, I am so overwhelmingly afraid to pass over it. What if the driver, who is obviously drunk by now, smashes into the bridge and we all drown! My fear is So overpowering that I grit my teeth and clench my fists. Elvis Costello is booming away in the background. I desperately feel like crying.

Their voices become louder and louder but I don't understand what they are saying. I know it's, about me. I relegate myself to quiet contemplation. An impossibility at this point. Now they are all singing. We arrive at one of the girls' brownstones and she asks if I want to join their sex party. The bile climbs up in my throat and I politely say no and retreat to my room. Next day, I feel is this some kind of joke? Did they bring me here to make fun of me? We stop off in Central Park. They light up more joints. By this time I am scared out of the daylight. Then to Coney Island we nearly hit a car. They ask me if I would like to go on a roller coaster. I say no but they pressure me. More for their amusement than anything else. I mingle with the crowd. Going home, every time we go over a bridge it's the same panic. After seeing Ferris wheels, bursting lights and loud music., I am ready to vomit. When the car finally arrives back home the nausea in me is released completely.

Chapter Six

Sitting in class next year the walls around me have grown bigger. I express affection to the two girls who have adopted me, by a playful punch on the upper arm. But I can't even tell who's who. I go through classes in a haze. I dream of living in a castle. For art project, I draw myself as a medieval princess. When report comes, instead of the A's and B's of last year, I am flunking out.

Chapter Seven

Today I see my psychiatrist, whom I have been seeing for quite a few months now. She doesn't seem to help. Her expressions seem fluid, changing like a chameleon from one to the next. She seems to be testing me. Or maybe she's not sure of who she is. I notice a piece of lint on the floor and pick it up, put it down and comment on it. I speak of my kingdom in glowing terms. I look at her and now she's suddenly frozen. The tape recorder continues. It bothers me. I speak some more but, like a foreigner—she asks me to explain myself. I feel I am being quite lucid. After an hour my mother picks me up. I stumble out into the cold winter air. Two days later my mother gives me an option upon advice of my doctor, either to spend Christmas with my father (who of course I have never met) an impossibility, or to go into a mental institution for Christmas. I become hysterical. What is this, some joke? My eyes burn with tears. I fly up into my room. There's nothing wrong with me!

Later on, my mother says I don't have to go into the hospital for Christmas, but rather the day after, despite my psychiatrist's request. I spend a lonely Christmas, none of it matters, none at all.

Chapter Eight

What would it be like to live in a castle? I am painting this green hills and more velvety green hills pour into each other, and at the end. Oh, please—a palace so beautiful it's silver turrets tear into the satin blue sky and the sun lazily hovers above, a pale yellow drop of lemon in this sea of azure. Now I will just add some doors, huge red doors and a brook running softly around its friend keeping a playful watch, yet a careful guard so as not to lose its presence. I inhale deeply the magic drug permeating my very pores. My throat suffocating, yet alive with the feel of this swirling grey ghost inside. The taste of the tissue—like paper twist firm against my lips and the hot red fire at the end, a fire fairly burning my fingertips.

Somewhere in my mind Genesis is playing "play me my song, here it comes again and again..." The Music Box. Hmm, it echos and fades away as images flood my mind.

I look up—I hold the canvas so huge in my pale boney fingers. My fingertips are stained blue, green, rust. I scrutinize. I am pleased.

I carefully place my fantasy against the far wall—the only vague reminder; accomplice in the crime. I secretly close the bedroom door behind me. Then the room is left to itself. Silent. I slide into my large navy down coat as the cold outside greets me strong against my body. The night. I walk and fumble at the deepness at my side for that very special thing. My feet are saying—I am taking you somewhere. But you'll never know. A second later I am miles away in the night and she is whispering seduction in my ears—the only warmth, that occasional warm glow caressing my lips. The sky is electric blue. The stars scream out—silence!

The road is filled with cars, so many cars going to and from, going this way and that. Their headlights their only witness to their bodies. The hundreds of suns blotching my coat and playing havoc with my image. Twisting the buildings and businesses on the side streets; which bow to the ground and magically float back, up.

God, how good I feel. I feel so alone. Nobody knows where I am now. Where I have gone. (I fantasize now.) The rush of traffic is dimmed only by the screech of brakes.

I turn my head back. Hesitantly. A large black limousine stretching like a cougar—creeps along silently beside me. (I can't—see the driver.) Its pale yellow eyes smile surreptitiously from the side. Automatically the door opens. I stop. A forlorn small bony figure, in an oversize coat, its hair tied back in a brown bun. I strain to see, what is inside. Clouds of smoke pour forth and then part.

A man, a beautiful man with creamy black hair and a hawk—like nose, nods to my prepossession. I am shy. I turn away slightly, never letting my eyes lose sight of their master. He gives me a tacitly understood nod as I feel myself drawn into the mammoth interior—a Plush silver—grey.

I sit comfortably within, and the beast drives on. My friend (somehow I remember him from another past) sits smoking a long cigarette holder of gold and silver never—ending. The brain of the beast is now in control of our destiny and my friend's hands rest celestially on his lap—some Ouija board he claims to possess under his delicate fingers. I ask him questions in my mind as they are answered almost imperceptively.

Soon the never—ending stream of cars creep into a forest of dreams. Ours is the one and only animal stalking some hidden prey. Trees of all kinds, interspersed take over the road which now becomes a dusty dirt path. The grossly deformed trees their arms outstretched to us welcome us, yet cry out for privacy in their need for a dark dwelling place. The sky—which only now becomes visible in patches, is soaring in pastels of orange, green, amber and blue. It seems multidimensional as the sun has now set and a quiet night takes over.

He looks at me, Emillio I'll call him. We are old—go back to long ago—yet like a new book so much remains unknown from one journey to the next. He eyes me, and I feel a glow inside which overwhelms all else. A closed smile of sympathy and understanding. And yet—the vehicle has stopped. I look around, open my eyes slowly—a smile of comfort upon my lips. My eyes shut, and never want the ride to end. I see that we are enveloped in a mirage miles ahead—through the clear stretch, I see the castle, our castle. The car is miraculously transformed into a shining black horse now, which we both find ourselves astride comfortably. His gallop is slow as I hold onto the smooth plushness of his sturdy stomach I feel the motion and the sound of his hooves. He says nothing. I can feel, as I look down, see the ground speeding ahead of us. The images, trees, sky and beautiful exotic plants whiz by. I close my eyes, and feel the pounding singular sensation of one. Soon as my eyes open and before me is the most perfect alabaster with beautiful pink veins running through, a palace so big, a silver knocker on the door and the finest pale wisps of grass peep through beneath my feet. Two bushes guard the entrance. I feel him lifting me off the horse—his strong hard forearms. His suit of black, his face a reminder of what is to come.

The home is intentionally done. Each room a decoration of a different culture and era. The main hallway is covered in beautiful oriental rugs. Tapestry of red and gold. The walls a breathtaking scene. I run my fingers over, the stiff texture. I feel the weight of my jacket and feel like a child. We sit in the room adjoining—a huge spacious room of antiques and jade, pottery, brass, pewter and sterling pieces, all around seem to magically fit in their appropriate places. And we drink wine.

His finger points to me and I realize I must go upstairs. Up the ascending carpeting. A spiral of stairs. In my room of white rugs and crystal chairs I find a diaphanous long gown of white—with every possible spectrum of the rainbow. I let it caress my face the waist and then my legs.

Downstairs the table is set. A nectar, one of the fruits is poured. I stare into his eyes and I feel a sick feeling inside me I have never felt before. After dinner we make love, a breathtaking spiritual communion.

Chapter Nine

The ride to the Institute of Pennsylvania Hospital, hospital, it reverberates in my mind like chewing hard candy when one bites down hard. The stinging sweetness provoking one to cough and choke. It is the day after Christmas. The doctor said that Christina should get to the hospital as fast as possible. Could this really be in emergency? I huddle in closely on the vinyl car upholstery. My mother driving on, her face intent. She grips the steering wheel with direction. My sister inanely babbles frightening questions. I know they don't like me, and I need an escape which I have. We round the curve, the cold cruel winter has taken heart. The stream—snaking its way around all, lies sedately. It's hard and frozen over, the currents buried fast, it's memory is a dream.

I smooth my face in desperate anxiety with my hands. The wrinkles seem to peel down and off. The hum of the motor vehicle almost piercing to my ears. How much longer? We wait in silent objectives.

It was a somber Christmas of many, many presents. My mother at her peak of generosity she is always so giving, that way.

We lull slowly in the city traffic now and cars seem to bump and collide with each other. The many colors have left muddied slush in their wake. Dear God—I am afraid, help me with this please. My mother is talking about the oil. I know she's referring to my dark roots. "Yes what is it darling?" I squirm. "No, nothing." It comes out like the penance of a soldier. But I am not to worry, soon I will be in that magical kingdom of mine, where all is quiet complentatude.

"Make a right here", my sister's voice oozing a sweet compassion.

Yes I know I am the sick one. I know the haunting crunch of gravel mixing with the car tires echoes in my mind. "Aren't you coming out Christina?" Deftly I take my wooden legs and throw them out of the car. The building is huge—in an old yellowed stucco. I carry my huge suitcase tripping with the weight of it. Mother looks for the door. Old brown, a huge—it says on the sign: "Experimental Psychology". But why did I come here? I had no choice—either to be thrown out of the house or find foster in this place.

Rounding the trodden lawn this intimate sanctuary is filled with blissful beauty, of all types of trees covered in a sparkling glaze. The front entrance, and huge white Doric columns. We step carefully up the white entrance and are warmed immediately by the stately beauty of the place. Georgian antique chairs and sofas—a spiral type staircase. Our voices play from wall to wall the entrance hall, so large.

As we speak with the receptionist, an elderly frail white woman, let fall into category with the long antiseptic hallway, slowly things begin to change. Up the elevator into a locked ward. We enter in. Eight people or so are wandering through the room. Some look up curiously, others oblivious to any and every world but their own. I tremble and smile at the interested ones. The door with one tiny window locks behind me. I am frightened. Help. I don't belong here. My God, I don't belong here.

A nurse gently touches my elbow, she looks like Catherine of Aragon. I don't like this at all. I am led to my room, a tiny bed the only obvious piece of furniture. I don't even have my painting supplies. These walls—she is speaking to me. What is she saying, I can't tell, she must speak a different language. Besides, she is one of those. A bad one. I know the patients are all talking about me. My mother leaves, silently and abruptly, I can't understand this—I am trapped forever. I know these nurses in the little glass box are talking about me. I sit down and pretend to read—yet I can't. I have to perfect this image—my gait is slow, my back perfectly straight—my clothes in perfect form and wander back to my bedroom where all is peaceful. I study the grayed dirty walls—but I can't cry and haven't been able for two years or so. So I see my castle. Oh beautiful one, how do you make these things possible. I go right off to sleep.

Chapter Ten

The cocoon is finely meshed—yet with no escape. One would liken the building more to a college dorm. Separate rooms, ping pong, t.v. and eating area. Sometimes the patients go for walks in a fenced in area. This particular day I jogged around the quarter—mile ground area, for I have been feeling terribly cooped in. As I sit on the bench, the patients slowly dissipate. Night grows ever so close... and fonder. The mauve silk seeping into the pink holes in the sky. The full moon just barely making itself known. I nestle up closer in my jacket and dream of my castle.

"I'm sorry miss, time to go in". The security guard offers me solace but I find none. My legs stiff from sitting too long, take me to the heavy metal door. I catch one last sight of her beauty and go in. Back on the unit, I hear George, "it's in the air, it's in the air!". Who could convince him otherwise. Apparently he's been strolling these halls for several years now. He rushes over to me, hand twiddling, eyes squinting, moving his head about in a jerky fashion. He's in his mid forties. He slides over, permitting me space to accompany him. "Oh goddess

Christina, do you want to hear about dynamism tonight?" I say no thank you. What am I doing here? I'm fine, I've just got to go out. The door has not been locked as of yet. The nurses are very busy tonight with Barbara. I hear the screams from the confinement room—I secretly steal out the door, run down three flights my shoes allowing a staccato echo and out into the yard. No one in sight, I bolt to the nine foot fence. The cold December air, the grass is crisp and fragile beneath my feet, overwhelms me. Silently I climb the fence, but my leg is—stuck—I tear at my pants leaving a large hole. The cars stream by me and the darkness engulfs me. But I am over—safety at last. I walk briskly under the El and head to Lovey's Lounge. The bar is filled with elderly black men. A large mirror and a juke—box sit quietly near the entrance. I put my money on the bar and I ask for a gin and tonic. Few pay any attention to me. I bolt the drink, down—and—start small talk with the man next to me.

Chapter Eleven

Today a special meeting has been called for one of the patients on one of the floors committed suicide. He hung himself. However other patients don't seem too upset about this. Some wear the stone faces of the gods of Easter Island, others cry—and some seem falsely inured to the situation. It seems the second suicide this week where earlier a young man threw himself through the barricade site of construction falling four floors to his death on the grating outside on North Field. (North Field is where all the patients can go for an outside walk.)

Chapter Twelve

I am ushered into a private glass room. It is called the fishbowl, all curtains are drawn. The room is filled with a few doctors, some nurses and the head doctor. The doctor looking so livid in this state. He sits and asks me to join him. The doctor is so tall and timid, his emaciated planes on his face taking on more definition as he talks. This man might try to hurt me. I am slightly caught off guard. I quietly place my body, lower it slightly, trembling, to the chair. My eyes cast downward. I don't need a psychiatrist. His questions continue. "Could you tell me a little about yourself?" My face sinks into disarray. I clam up. I feel my hands like great rocks. My heart pounds so loudly I'm sure all can hear. I pause. I answer. The doctor to me: "You don't have to make such excuses, use such big words, why are you afraid?" I stand up exactly and leave the premises. I hear a tapping behind me as a young nurse draws me back within the room. The session seems to last forever. Question after question, pounding and pounding. My new doctor, the attending, seems to stare at me unblinkingly. It seems a great conspiracy, unrelinquishing. After what seems an eternity, I am guided back through the units locked door, into the lounge where patients are watching t.v., and others look stigmatized, mechanized as they shuffle across the floor, fingers twiddling, faces twitching. Not my world, I would never take medication.

Chapter Thirteen

Six A.M.—restless in my sleep, The nurses wake up call disturbs me not. In my small room with one barred window, I dress in the deep chill, my body shivering all over. Then the knock on the door to verify "Are you up Christina?". I answer back a throaty yes. As I sit on my bed and observe with great clarity the lack of privacy, everything in the room is unbreakable—one could never harm oneself. There are "checks" as one enters the floor and strip searches too!

I wander out of my room, rubbing my eyes, face and forehead. Some of my friends greet me in their strange language. We all sit down in a special room with each table for four people, and are served institutional food. Today cereal sausage and milk. (Patients are to fill out menus beforehand.) The banter is not devoid of humor, nor is it stingingly sharp, but rather, difficult to understand.

Morning meeting there are five or so of us concerned with the subject of mice because of construction. Is Karen hallucinating I argue, other people have seen mice too. I break in, "If the head administrator doesn't do anything about it, I will call the board of health". I feel like one of the patients who is able, and will stand up for her rights. Morning meeting is dismissed. I return to pacing up and down the halls. I see Wendy coming toward me in her Gucci shoes and Louis Vittone handbag. She catches my eye. "Christina", she says in a secretive tone, "look at this". I enter her room and see, that her bed is swathed in toilet paper! "I am going to set fire to this place so we can all escape." "Oh, no Wendy, I almost interrupt, "you can't do that". I rush over to the nursing station. Within minutes, the fire department arrives and all is under control.

Chapter Fourteen

Another night has strung by. Vivid and in repose, I wake to the footsteps echoing in the hallway and strange voices off-setting the calamitous thoughts swirling in my mind, trouble and turmoil. A loud rap at the door jolts me to my senses as I beckon the person in. A very tall young woman, Darleen, with a theatrically made up face and bright neon clothes gesticulates in a foreign way that today she has planned a group of us to go rafting. Twelve of us are gathered like lamb for the slaughter-house. Bewildered expressions like store-bought mannequins, and some with no expression at all, their faces a blank slate. I nudge my friend Barbara as we all gather to the van. The many hour—like drive leaves some calm and some not so calm as if awaiting some horrible fate. I absorb the beauty of the passing verdant hills and flowers with quiet surrender. My friend Barbara and I seep in the scenery and make noble banter. Soon we enter a tree-filled entrance. Hearing the sound of gravel on the pathway fills my head with sensations of so many years past when as a child I attended pre-school. I reminisce and drop the thoughts as a rude awakening of Darleen's loud rasping voice. She calls us out of the van in condescending tones. We file out and wait, like children, to be told what to do next. We all gather and walk to a large vast area where there a many large rafts. We sit. The director explains what must be done. Enthusiasm begins to bring some of the patients to life. We are divided into groups. Darleen, John (an unclean very heavy man in his thirties), Barbara (my friend of my age) and I. As we look over the great expanse of water we are held in awe of nature's beauty. All kinds of trees tower above. We launch off. The sun blinding our eyes, reflects off the water and finds warmth for the mottled trees surrounding us. The waves devour our raft, while we paddle through this undulating snake as best as we can. When bang we become wedged on a rock. Darleen with her great height begins to push. Barbara and I help. We push to no avail; while John sits in the raft with a glazed expression asking, while each raft goes by, if any one of the passing rafts "has a light" for his cigarettes. I stifle my laughter.

Going home we stop off at a pizza place. I feel the grogginess settling upon myself as the van crawls over the bumpy road. I feel the difficulty keeping my eyes open, however the bluest electric blue sky gains my attention. I am transported to my youth when I was five years old and used to run up the street to my friends. The fear that used to enthrall me, kept my small legs running a straight path till I found comfort within his domicile.

Chapter Fifteen

After spending seventeen months in North Building, I am finally ready to move to center building and then possibly... leave.

All the hours upon hours of therapy leaves me better but not too much so. Was it just the contained environment, away from the family, the family council, a dictatorship which delegates lashes upon lashes for what they could consider bad behavior?

I came into the institute like a frustrated child, but really more psychotic. I lived in castles, slept conscious with the night and worshiped my own personal, changing reality.

The gurney speeds down the hall, my belongings hastily stacked above. I witness the carpeted floors. How different from the dry institutional setting of North Building. I check into the nurses station and meet the new people. No more morning meetings, or being physical harassed. I walk past the lounge and see the saloon doors to my room. Nice furniture, a mirror, lamps. My eyes show soft approval. I feel my tired body reeling to the bed. With my eyes staring at the ceiling, I realize that this is the first time that I've really felt safe.

After being in the hospital after eighteen months, I feel a need to get out and do something. It just so happens, that my mother found a clipping in the paper for Liberty Belle tryouts. (Philadelphia Eagle's football cheerleading tryouts.) My sister comes to take me and she shows me the cutout in the paper. Why not? It would make me feel worth something. I ask for a pass for that day but don't say for what for. My sister picks me up. I struggle to take out my curlers in the car and put on my make-up. Soon we are there and find the correct entrance. My stomach walls closing in and my heart palpitating. The spacious stadium is packed with hundreds of beautiful girls. Nine-hundred in all. There are twenty positions to fill. We are sorted into groups and file down to the Astro-turf. The colors abound like a carnival. First a group of five or so walk in front of the judges table (consisting of celebrities). the driving beat of the disco music fills and swarms in the air, the five girls do their best free style dancing. After waiting for several more groups to go, I am nervous but remember to smile and project, my legs trembling. Some of the girls are taken out, some, more and more. Till finally a group of fifty, their numbers being called out over the loud speaker. My God! I made it. But these are just the preliminary tryouts. (There were several of these "cuts".)

I go back to the hospital and keep it all to myself, each pass or day I go to the Vet to learn the tryout routine. One night I think everybody there was talking about me. The voices sticking at me like needles from all directions, I run out. I hear my choreographer, her voice echoing in the hall of the stadium. "Where are you going?" I reply, "I feel sick" and got out as fast as possible. Most of my unknown paranoia I try to keep to myself. The rest of the night I spent wandering the streets of Philly. Days were spent practicing and practicing the routine taught to us. I go back to the hospital and practice in front of the mirror.

Soon the big day arrives at the Tyler School of Art. My transportation gets mixed up and I ended up having to hitchhike halfway there. My heart pounding I make it there just in time. The girls push and shove to get their makeup on in the back, room. Then, five of us file on stage to the primitive beat of "Funky Town". Will I remember the routine? Will I remember the moves? After what seems like eons, there is a quiet hush. The winner's names are announced and presented with a yellow rose. I am one of them! I walk home alone wishing to share my triumph with someone.

Chapter Sixteen

As I wind my way through the tiled halls, the bowels of the building, (to see my doctor) I think back on previous sessions. The man seems more interested, not particularly in a humanistic way, though, in me. He says "come in." I enter. His office is plush. One's eyes first fasten on the large fish tank with the piranhas, the cushy couch and chairs and of course the paintings on the wall. Today he lies ensconced on the sofa and speaks to me like a Roman popping grapes. His casualness seems to construe an uncanny nature though into the months I had been here, he has not prescribed medication. Sometimes we have family meetings in this way, but only a couple. He repeatedly tells me I am "becoming a woman" although I have been diagnosed schizophrenic, he won't put me on anything. Our topics are seldom heavy, although later in the day there's a feeling of accomplishment. He managed to break down my superficiality somewhat.

Chapter Seventeen

After being discharged from IPH, I find an apartment and a job after being permitted to live at home for a few months. Working at the Ramara Inn, is an impossible job for me learning all the details and putting them into motion. The boss is yelling at me now. Customers are watching. My blushed face, the tears about to come. Am I so dumb? Why can't I hold this job down? The phone rings, it's my Mother. "Yes mom. An astral projection convention?"

"Faydra Etemad."

I don't understand, why is my mother asking me to go to this? Saturday, 1:00 pm. I show up at the convention held in an unstately large room of the Ramara. I was chosen ahead of time, to hand out pamphlets to those attending. I smile at each strange face and hand out the brochures. Fifty or so people must be there. We all sit down. Faydra walks from the back of the room to the front and is glitterized in her blue satin revealing dress, her gold bangles and baubles sparkling wildly in her eyes and her heavy stage makeup. She begins by telling us what astral projection is, then how to do it. We all lie on the floor breathing deep breaths in synchrony. Several people ask questions. I know they are all referring to me. There! One of the women turns around to look at me and acknowledges that they are. They are discussing my future, that I am going to a university and on my way to one of my classes I am shot by a terrorist. I feel sick to my stomach. How could this be? After the show the performer and her two sons drive me home. The car is filled with sexual innuendo and perversion. I yell to them. It must be I I or 12 at night. The streets are dark and foreboding but somehow I get, out, slam the door of the gold Cadillac and run the rest of the way home. I rush up to my room and listen to a talk show to calm down. What are they saying? The man's chafed voice resounds out. "… and these adolescent derelicts are feeding off the people." His voice like the first clap of a thunder storm, I tune into the show. They are talking about me! Being compared to an adolescent derelict—I feel a harshness; no part in society. I gather all my change together, go outside to the nearest pay phone. The streets are scary. I call the station. I am on the air. "But what exactly is an adolescent derelict?" The tears filling my throat. He is mean and abrupt. "Listen miss, if you have got something wrong with your head you'd better get it fixed." I return to my small efficiency and feel deathly afraid to even touch that dial again. You see, I live in the city alone and have to. I know something is wrong but I don't know what.

Chapter Eighteen

I have always admired and I should say respected such low, down dives like Ribits, 2nd and Front close to the Delaware River. It's doors a garish stain-glass panel. A perfect tourist trap for one who wants to eat cheaply, relax in a vinyl booth and carry on with highly made-up waitresses. (Who, incidentally are not earning for school but to merely meet, greet and hopefully marry.)

On this particular drizzly afternoon I arrived at Ribits, ready to tackle my job as hostess in a somewhat shall we say "impromptu" way. The heel on one of my pumps—had a breakdown, and the hobble from Septa bus to the bar/restaurant was akin to balancing on golf tees. With my grand appearance, hair in strings and expensive Saks Fifth Avenue pants soaked halfway up (my only pair) I was told sweetly by the manager to go home (roughly 21 blocks), change, and report back. I felt perhaps, maybe just a belly bauble would be appropriate not counting inches upon inches of peacock blue mascara. (To match of course.) However, so be it. I came back dressed to the hilt. Tailored silk blouse (Altmans), beige wool skirt (Saks), fine pearls (with the knots between of course) and flat shoes, It was really obviously "the gams" he was after.

My mind being, in such a flight I was busy smiling, hostessing each crude brand of clientele back and forth, table to table, somewhat like baggage. In the midst of my duties one of the more congenial waitresses approached me. "There is a man in the first booth who wishes to see you as soon. as you finish with your customer."

I nodded. A strange sensation crept over me which I will liken to the chills. I rounded the bend and found to my surprise a little shriveled man absorbed in the black vinyl booth. His brown velvet blazer, matching pants and crocheted yellow tie made a very curious combination. He eyed me directly through his large brown tortoise shell glasses which obscured his tiny face and streamlined features. He extended his right arm stiff with a closed smile and presented himself "Hello my name is Emillio Rosa." He articulated in a thick English accent, as he presented his card. "I would like to have drinks with you around 5:30. Meet me at the Mexican consulate—located on the 4th floor of the Bourse building."

What could I say? I found him ugly yet strangely attractive. I smiled. And while holding his card in my most sophisticated voice I could muster, spat out— "Oh that would be lovely. Thank you very much." (How literate can one get?) And that was that. The rest of my day flew by. After all, I had something to look forward to—didn't I? The customers slowly chewed their last morsels. I grew impatient in the comer, snuck back to the kitchen for a few last fries, and it was time to go.

I donned my beige "London Fog" and stepped out onto the slanted slippery pavement. The wind was demonic, and I slowly winded my way to the Bourse Building.

After finding the right floor, I realized I was in yet another ghost town, everyone had left. But would he be there? The idea of being stood up disgusted me so. However, down the corridor, after passing one anti-septic door like the next, my eyes caught sight of a large, shall we say plate, on the door. Hmm. "Consulado de Mexicano". Look, flags and animals and a wreath of something. God—wouldn't it just be easier for them to put on a rather large brightly colored sombrero, something at, least that was comprehensible.

I realized at this point what I had delved into, by my acceptance. Two timid raps on the door as the door slid open quietly on dark carpeting. My eyes rose, and there was Emillio. A little gnome. "Come in—Christina."

I was determined, as my eyes first fastened in the spacious room, on rows upon rows of books—to be seen, at least as an intellectual.

He strode his long, skinny, proportioned five foot one inch body across the room. I was directed into a place of fifty or so chairs in an oval. "This is where we have our conferences." Then—an office taste-fully done with a bright sunny window. Emillio Rosa stood behind the large padded business chair resting each hand on top.

I searched for a wedding band—well, so far so—but what's this a stained glass pinky ring. Gulp.

We engaged in some little dance of I am this, you do that—vice verse, etcetera, etcetera.

"Well", his tone was stern. "I believe it's time to go."

We walked side by side out into the rain. something told me that he was very wealthy. As I suspected he suggested we hail a cab. I quickly intervened— "No Emillio let's take the bus". We madly waved after one of these long awkward things, and caught it just in time. The bus was empty. The white blue lights casting a lazy glow. I have never seen anybody seem so fearful in my life. His feet dangled a foot and a half above the floor, and his arm steadied his body from either side, as we bounced up and down at the back of the bus. He couldn't have looked more scared.

Soon we got out—"Fillys Cafe". (Country and western bar.) A smattering of people were plucking their feathers, boasting their chest's and Emillio and I luckily found two backless bar stools together. A twangy guitar was permitting conversation. Emillio asked me in a very businesslike tone what I would like. Somehow, groping through the cobwebs of my mind, I remembered! "A gin and tonic please." (A drink of sophistication.)

After my drink arrived and our conversation grew more and more stiff between Emillio and I, I realized with quiet abruptness that we were surrounded by three very tall men. Emillio was playfully, busily, exchanging phone numbers and making dates? With these pals? I tried to sip my gin and tonic, however I'm sure that if any olive had been in the drink someone, one of—his friends, would have to have performed the Heimlich maneuver on me!

Emillio asked me if I was "going to ride the bull" of the mechanical sort. I gritted my ivory whites and smiled ruefully. "No thank you, but I appreciate your asking."

Emillio stood up, and I realized it was time to go. (At least he could have allowed me a jeweled collar like poodles have!)

Out of the stuffiness and into the gradually darkening day. Not a word was uttered from the taxi, soon we stopped at 22nd and Spruce. As I fell out of the taxi Emillio put up his umbrella of beige, rust and black. This umbrella was so large (a beach umbrella) I feared we would literally "bump" other pedestrians off of the walk and into the street.

But I was proud. I loved his height, his long thin legs, brown cap of hair, and round blue eyes, his rosebud lips and of course it all reminded me of someone, but I couldn't place who. However, I knew he was special.

Past the curiosity shops, the pizza parlor, Emillio popping his head in jovially. "Hello Bill business going well?" He seems so happy. I was glowing inside and out.

Rounding the comer, things began to look hauntingly familiar. A tall Robert Redford passed by us—he looked down on us with kindly eyes the way one would view a child with his favorite stuffed animal. I felt sick—I wanted Emillio not to see. But, too late. A few more steps and the key was inserted in the lock of a large brownstone—21st and Spruce. "Emillio you know, I think. I mean, I live here, two blocks away." No response. The question was carried off with nonchalance. Mister Rosa led the way up the two flights. I followed. Outside of his apartment was a crystal chandelier lamp. He opened the brown door and we walked in. Institutional food would have tasted better—the grey undecorated walls sent a chill from one spacious end of the square to the next. (Thank God the paint wasn't peeling.) Through the small entrance hall and into the rectangle of a room, a kite of red and white, a paper fish, hung apathetically on the wall no more in place than to cover a stain. A small, small square mirror to the left—below a stack of twenty or so albums.

A small stereo, and in the middle of the room facing the two windows, a comfortable worn sofa for two and a low coffee table, confessing subordinacy to the more proud sofa. I sat on the left of the sofa, and Emillio presented two comical goblets which, before I could say anything, were filled with red wine. I dared not drink it for fear of ending up in a coma. On the sofa with Emillio, wearing my expensive Saks skirt which I certainly wouldn't have. We talked, I don't remember what about. In reverie, I slowly glanced down at the "thing" on the coffee table. "Emillio?" My voice escaped childlike. "What is that, those pliers for?"

"Oh Christina—didn't I tell you? They're my tools."

I feared for my life and just somehow intuitively knew not to question further.

Somehow—that evening, we ended up in bed. Emillio, propped up in a squaw position, playing with his remote control; and Benny Hill making fiendish faces doing advertisements for Frederick's of Hollywood. I, useless of course grabbed only what was in sight. A glamour magazine a few points short of Cosmopolitan—the bedside bible, but I managed to force my eyes from one strange black shape to the next. What was next, could only be adored. We each stripped down to our underwear, and I sitting lazily on the corner of his waterbed, (a fear of relaxing too much because of maybe being swallowed up in the murky depths and or strangled by seaweed). Emillio took off his shirt revealing a taut, tan chest. He stripped down to his underwear—at which point he presented himself in full form. As I admired his body—I could almost feel myself—the sculptor, molding each gracious curve.

Then, he leaned forward—each hand on either side of me, I wanted to kiss him so badly. However, my desire manifested itself as a mere titter, which became giggles and of course the denoumont, guffaws.

He shot back in shock, after departing to the living room—I left him in peace, and his nerves soothed. When he came back into the bedroom, he presented me with a token of his affection. A pair of wonderful white Carters underwear (the classical kind). I gracefully accepted. them, carefully folded them and trotted off to my flat.

As I sat in my apartment—I pondered the situation (should I try on the sordid thing?) and wanted to give him something in return. After climbing through my wardrobe—the cotton jungle, I found my sizzler dress (purchased early on in my crazed adolescence). This is the kind a la Marilyn Monroe, whereby if you happen to be caught in a gale wind—you have something to show for it: matching undies! This particular breed was nylon. Somewhat conservative with pastel pink and blue scribbly flowers all over. And now for the finishing touch—I took a black magic marker and added a black smiley face on the right buttock.

I sealed the envelope appropriately and ran up the evening street to his apartment. I left the little nuisance in his mail box for all to see.

A few days passed, no reply. A couple more days. I can't wait any longer. Off to Chaucers.

I dolled up my hair, perfected my makeup, and put on my four inch heels and baggies and an Indian necklace I made. All complete.

The look of an artist.

Chaucers is an old English pub—complete with pinball machines and Pac-man. I swung open the heavy door my heart pounding.

Emillio sat at the far end of the bar in a black leather jacket—pants and his elevator shoes. I cautiously approached him. Not so much as a glance my way—however, I proceeded. I hesitantly bent forward to whisper in his ear. "Emillio did you get my, uh, underwear?" He stared at me then—with those two blue saucers, and said for ALL to hear—"Yes Christina, I got your underwear and I had the bomb squad check it out!"

I felt like a rose—the kind you would send a lover—in full bloom. My cheeks burned so red seductively fled out of Chaucers into the street, sat on the curb at the intersection and shook with laughter.

Chapter Nineteen

Rich is mortified and filled with fury, he knows about Emillio yet when I insist on making a phone call to him—he looks at me with angry red eyes and what looks like he's about to crush the earth in one blow. I hasten out the door, my feet padding down the worn wooden stairs (the yellowed light making me feel I am in some strange interrogation room. I hate this place. The walls crumbling and poverty possessing from the floor to the ceiling) and out of his apartment. As if I am on fire I walk one block enjoying the crisp summer air. But what's this, a taxi cab is on fire, given up its purpose on the side of the street. Emillio is it you? Are you… My mind squirms with anguish. What can I do now? Can I help him? I begin to run toward the cab the police gently sending me back. I catch sight of the occupants who are now out of danger. Neither one Emillio. The police have already arrived so I can do nothing. All I feel is a rage of anger that it could have been Emillio (or anyone at all) and these people are just—standing. Gawking. I want to yell and scream at them and burst and spit ferocity at them. But soon enough as they are told, the vultures flock, I'm sure, to another tasty sight. I run home the next five or six, blocks and reach in my pocket for a dime. My purse! Where is my purse? Oh—I, I must have left it at Rich's. The conclusion slapping me in the face. I run back up, I rush through the decrepit door. That's right, I left it downstairs on the radiator, outside of that apartment. I knock on their door, first they all ask if they can help me. I see men and women dressed in negligees, some sort of strange goings on. They say they don't have my purse. I thank them, slamming the door. I run to my apartment, up four flights, and knock, on my neighbor's door. She unlatches it carefully and says, "Who is it?" "It's Christina," She peeks out then slowly opens her door. I explain the situation to her. Yes I may use her phone.

"Hello Emillio." Blank, then "Oh… it's you," a dry, answer. "Could you help me?" I speak raggedly for I am out of breath. "I've lost my handbag and need, to borrow some money for a new lock." He hangs up the phone. I feel my insides turn sour. But this is nothing new, he has always treated me that way. I walk back to Rich's and the people on the bottom floor have found my purse all intact!

Chapter Twenty

Eight P.M. I am in my apartment. The pill (speed) is fast going down; all I can think of is Emillio. I wander into my tiny adjoining bathroom and stare at my face in the mirror. The mascara, eye shadow, and lipstick, stand out like the marked face of a mandarin. Is it right to appreciate beauty in this way—or to give up the materialistic things of this sunken earth world? I recline back in spiritual wonderment—I feel a high. I wash every last remnant off my face vowing never to wear the dirtied muck again. For a voice has told me not to wear the filth. It's now three A.M. and the night has just begun. I think of Emillio, how he mistreats me. I see a vision in my mind and go, to putting it on paper.

   (1) Emillo was gullible and red.
   (2) His father told him time to bed.
   (3) He crept up to the attic so near.
   (4) And stole a punch of prisoner fear.
   (5) He fastened it then, to his toe.
   (6) Its purple ebullience—it did glow!
   (7) But mother ghost called from downstairs.
   (8) And as he rasped to call her near.
   (9) He fell down from her apron string.
  (10) And tore his ankle, splintering.
  (11) She guessed the miss, but called no one.
  (12) But as both died for father's son.
  (13) For father's son.

In explanation: Lines 1-4; You see Emillio drinks a lot, and when around his over domineering father, he thinks of being physical with him (such nasty thoughts we desire).

Lines 4-5; But instead he stubs his toe on the stairs for thinking the thought of abusing his father.

Line 6; However, Emillio admires this because of the beguiling thought.

Line 7; Soon his mother calls to see if he's all right and as he called her near, (he fell down he lost sight of her maternal nature).

Lines 9-10; A role she represents. He broke his ankle on the stairs.

Line 11; She knew what happened and wanted to help but she did nothing for fear of her husband's wrath.

Line 12; As Emillio's father cared for him too but in a different way.

3:15 A.M. Yes Emillio indeed has problems. I feel the need to write of his persona.

Chapter Twenty-One

I push open the heavy downstairs door from my apartment and walked out into the warm night. She swarms around me, the sights and sounds kept under a clear summer sky. I hear my feet tap past Emillio's apartment. I glance up unknowingly but see only his dried fern hanging in the window through the ghostly greenish glow. Rounding the curve I begin to jog. I feel a relentless surge of energy and see Rittenhouse Square nearby. I know I look ugly in my white T-shirt and cotton baggie shorts. My white legs with the veins so prominent. Noticeable. But this is right, God should have it this way. I'm sure he is pleased. For all through high school and out, I have worn make-up. This facade, no more. I feel that everyone—all in Philly, are watching and will soon gossip about this new state. My walkman is playing Genesis, as I jog to the Art Museum I find a cement wall with a hole in it. I stare at the expanse of sky lying there for what seems eons, as I contemplate Emillio, life, different philosophies etcetera. But across the lot, there is this minister who is getting out of his car. I have no fear. We gaze at each other from quite a distance like two animals assessing each other. Each holding the other one's reason to be there. At this place, at this time in mockery. He seems to want to protect me. The delusions start— he walks, his hands gesticulate in a strange fashion. Maybe this means I am going to lose my legs. I sit up disturbed and run towards home. A girl with her leg in a cast seems to know, though I am behind her, that I will lose my legs. My position in life. My eye begins to sting. I am too staunch for that. They well up in tears flooding my pristine cheek. I run so fast that I can barely breathe. It begins to rain.

Chapter Twenty-Two

The car is revving in the drive as my two sisters had planned to pick me up to see Norris, my father. They wave cheerful hellos. I have never seen him, though maybe as an infant perhaps. My christening being right around the divorce. I feel excited, though quite numb. This venture really means nothing to me. I sit in the back, seat with my safety—belt on. My thoughts travel at a quick speed. When we reach Boston, excitement seems to stir the air and what was once idle chatter has metamorphasized into important discursive talk. The mood has become much more rushed and serious. We pass two historical monuments, the scenery a dull escape from what we are about to face. I look at myself in the mirror trying desperately to remember my face so I can compare it to his. We all put on touch ups of make-up, a hint of lipstick, etcetera. We giggle like kids. We walk in the doctor's office. The man who had cheated my mother out of her alimony never once visited us, me now 19. The secretary leads us in, he is not expecting us. We walk in. Something about his face is blank, expression lost. He carries a list-lessness about him. An uncaring, unfeeling way. My two sisters sit in chairs facing his desk. I sit in the back of the room. They talk on and on, my two sisters chatting amicably. I am stunned. I find the experience so unrewarding that I just sit and stare. Toward the end of the hour he asks, frowning to me, "Doesn't she talk?" in a tilted tone. The room is filled with silence. When my two sisters ask him out to dinner, he gives a thorny response, no. As we leave, rejected, the three of us find what looks like the end of a park. We have what little food there is to eat, mostly oranges and bread, and we speculate on who he looks like. Why was he so old looking? It looks as though he were on drugs. We chew and gesture almost pushing our rejection off onto feeling sorry for him. Why did this happen to us? After our Meal as the twilight approaches we happen by his house. Shielded by a large tree, we see him arrive home from work to his wife of 19 years and children. A stooped little sad figure emerges from his green car. A beautiful blond girl and young man come out to do something with their car in the driveway. He enters his house. When we arrive home the next week, we find a letter awaiting us, telling my mother to "...never send your children up here again or I will send for the police to I come to take them away—Norris Alexander.—"

Chapter Twenty-Three

Today President Reagan is coming to the city. I put on my best white corduroys and jacket. Will I make it there? I run all the way to be greeted by mobs and mobs of people. Breathless, I begin to preach to the people. "Love Jesus," emphatically. "All you have to do is love Jesus." I moved from block comer to block. Three tough looking men caught my eye then stared. They yell at me "Just who are you talking to!," their tone abrasive and filled with malice. They angle their bodies in a position to strike. I fear for my life. During Reagan's speech I wandered between all the people. "Now this is what we are going to do... believe." Stressing the last word. I see anger in the crowd's eyes and they push animalistically to see the President enter his hotel at the end of the speech. I yelled to the crowd from the front of the police line. "Love, that's all you need!", my voice becoming harsh. "Now when President Reagan comes by we'll all shout LOVE." I spoke with a young fellow next to me. He is very nice but his blatant curiosity makes me feel strange, like an insect under the probing eye of a scientist. Teaching the masses, I felt that was the least I could do for Emillio. Soon a head appears, it is President Reagan's. As he looms into full view, my heart pounds. The crowd begins to hiss and boo. I am shocked. My voice saying one last "Love!". My body being almost caught about in the swaying of the suffocating masses. The tears begin to stream down my face. Why, oh why, can't people be kind?

Chapter Twenty-Four

Today I will go for a walk. It must be nine or ten evening with, I let chill air to envelop me. The city scares me. Chaucer's again. No one in sight, the telephone poles I pass by as people. I now run my fingers through my hair of ages. I must look right—be wearing the outfit that people like, accept the most. Will he be there? Some sort of yes. Dirtied muck in my brain. And I pray for him. Dear Emillio, I have never met anyone like you before. I love the way your hair cuts so closely—a mask about your head. Ready to shield at the slightest moment—pretense. But why are you standing there—hanging flopped on the bar stool in black like a pink ballerina hung by the neck—that (threat) umbrella around your neck must weigh a fortune often enough. "Emillio, are you all right?" The whispered fragment coursing in my mind as until it doesn't come out. A thorn in my heart; my, I stand gasping for air.

I can't watch this any longer—my brain has turned to jelly. I grow faint, my legs grow faint. I stumble out, feet to the ground. Each minute pattern of carpeting tracing me to the door. The laughter shatters the stained glass venetian lamps. All at once... they move. I cry inside—while God tries to pluck this thorn in my heart. I don't see you—where the hell' are you? I feel the tears in his eyes—not even letting, letting his eyes to stray, need to strain, turn from this place. Please. There, you see? I don't.

Chapter Twenty-Five

I found these flowers you see. Through and through torture and torment, embittered—I found them. The petals as red as the velvety grown from which each of them individually stemmed and oh—the thorns how sweet they are they're none. However I now have a bunch of these pretty pieces—I hold them loosely at my side, their scattered scrambled stems bridge them up closely to my face. The wind caresses them on to me. The aroma acrid yet a blissful ascent from the lingering twilight fumes which an occasional car will pass by me. No—there is no acknowledgement from Emillio, yet I will see today, if his inside door is locked. Empty of thought, or has someone left it open. Just for me. It was he who must have left it ajar. The rectangular brass piece holding the whole of it. The beautifully etched large old-fashioned panel of glass with wood mahogany frame. I am forthright overjoyed. I climb the steps—a child, two at a time, maybe stumbling on one, my hands sweaty in their overjoy of clenching the strangled greens. Cardboard pieces, are now soaked from my creased perspiration. At last—the last plane and I have arrived. His door is shut. A quiet peace—like being. He acknowledges to me. A few harmonic sounds enter forth from his door. He has his guitar now. Lonesome piano he plays. And I defy not the questions. He must know now, I am out here. His song is sad and plaintive—a sandpiper who in the middle of life, has had his leg injured and is no longer able to keep up with himself—the rest of his flock. Able to run freely or gracefully through the sun or feel the cool ocean at his feet, fingertips.

I quietly open his brass golden door knocker and place all my withered friends to sleep, their heads bowed together over their own fence—for him.

Quietly then I escape. Thoughtlessly and remotely.

Chapter Twenty-Six

This morning as I wake up I wash a long hard night fraught with nightmarish images and people trying to destroy me. My dreams have been this way since I can remember. After soothing myself in a very warm bath I feel an urge to go outside. It is a warm summer's day. As I put my clothes on, look in the mirror—a little voice I hear in my mind, one of the female consciences that has been guiding me tells me to get out and preach. Me, but why me? She stresses in secretive tones that I am the second Christ—or will be if I fulfill my duties. A great fear envelopes me. I hurry out, the door causing a cool blast in my face. I walk up two blocks from my apartment. With each passerby I ask if I can "help" them. Most quietly say no, some ridicule it with sexual innuendos. They all seem petrified, so intent with petty worries and stark reality. Why don't they consider Jesus as utmost? After standing on the corner for a few hours or so, my legs grow restless. I wander toward the imposing hospital where my sister works. As I near the front entrance, my sister in her white uniform, stops me at the door. She was having her lunch on the wall nearby. Obviously not of the body. "What are you doing?" The words ring in my ear reverberating loudly. I tell her calmly, "I am here to preach to the patients." She obviously doesn't understand. "You can't do that!" she says in a restraining voice. I walk through the doors, my sister rushes in behind me, "Security guard!" It rings out ignorance (she has a brief encounter with him). "I'm sorry Miss, but you will have to leave." He is an imposing man with dark features, an unceaseless stern quality about him. "But I have to preach to the people so that they will get better," my voice oozing compassion. He ushers me out quietly. I feel a deep sadness that neither one understands.

Chapter Twenty-Seven

I have been sitting in my apartment—a day like any other. My mind circles and flies above Emillio a demon dream, one lousy wicked thought—and, (of course) a host of others. Birds of prey—I pray for him at all costs. His life means more to him then, at all, except God and Jesus of course. I can imagine him in my mind stepping into cab. Forget of him Christina, for he is too foreign to co-exist with me.

I touch the graveling, grueling of the brownstone, holding its midst up to the sky. A perfect tower of strength. Oh, how I love him. Today I will go for a walk. The fool on the hill, I had that poster as a child, he looks so happy.

There's Mr. Lamont in his gallery, sitting behind his business desk, his weird wonderful works of convoluted art. Fiery zebras and sunken warriors. Flowers about to burst, Jesus strung on a cross. The sweat pours from my brow. How great it would be to meet him. Emillio No—not really. I don't mean that, how wonderfully love I would be. I reminisce. Scattered throughout his attic—I wonder if Mr. Lamont would accept my art pieces, render them necessary. A black and white abstract I could do that. Maybe. My feet press on. Pedestrians look at me, I smile God how thankful I am to be alive. Past the 7-11 borrowed cafe. (Life is slow and cool today like molasses tainted with sugar.)

I skip up gleefully the perfect cement steps outside the Dorchester—what a dream to live here.

I meet the street. Cars crawl and whiz across this particular intersection. Some slowly, their eyes beckon down some senselessly go through and on to on, I can almost predict how each car will go. A turn. Wealth. Love. Together as one. I hope. I feel funny, a cab pulls up to me. Out of the blue. Emillio must be at work now. It must be one or two in the afternoon. He steps purposefully up out of the cab. Does he pay the driver I am stunned. There he is. Can I catch you, you wicked butterfly? But his wings have been clipped. He is ten feet from me, headed toward me. Out of the cab now. Face to face. Mine, as dried glue,

"Hello Emillio." Now I beam from arch to arch. How his crocheted tie feels so much in my hands. I caress it over and over. We stand a breath away. He stammers from foot to leg, his knees bent, he can't even look me straight in the eye. Christina, Christina." He speeds up (I can't take this any longer). "Christina."

"Yes Emillio?" my face the edge of a smile amiss. He trembles—I smile. Slowly. All is calm, how the ocean has ceased above God's hands.

"I have something I want to tell you."

"Yes Emillio?" Again the breeze through and through the two of us—his blue veiled moments spinning eternities on our mind.

He tosses off, and spills into the dense mist of the cab. I follow after him not missing a bet. His and ours. We wrestle with the time and juggle each other's perceptions, now as one. Off the end of the block! Up until now silence. I feel for him. I look love at him, my theatrically made up face, blond wisps of hair glinting from my brow. And I say quietly, "Give me a kiss Emillio." His nervousness is gone now. The touch of a dove's feather—I get out and he drives away.

Chapter Twenty-Eight

I can't seem to forget you. Oh has haze, it was that afternoon, evening, when I followed you up those steps to your flat—I was blinded by your perfume. And why do you always wear those same clothes? The velvet attire of a junky prince.

3:00 afternoon, a bright sunny July day has us. Emillio I know we never really talked although I feel, somehow know, that your father is Mexican, your mother French. What do they look like—did you inherit your peaceful good looks from your mother? Your slender body and perfect thighs. Oh, how I remember them. Those eyes and nose of yours, your nose a delicate triangle set to calm seas. Other lands, better lands unto itself (two huge blue eyes). Your rounded brow—only open for me to touch it if and when the time is right, to caress the round hill, feel the baby-soft perfect furrow, as I soothe your every anxiety away with a cool, white cloth. Oh how I love you. And how good God has been to give good to me, to know of you too. A triangular soft lantern jaw.

You sit there so calmly—sedately in your chair, and your two frail velvety arms crossed. Never inching off the sofa. And your body only moving forward at the earliest prerequisite. A laugh, tiny beautiful rainbow bubble inside, reaching to travel out from your precious tongue.

Your wisdom is in words—not only the speech with which you hardly utter. I love you. Again and again, I love you.

Are we going but tonight Emillio, will I see, you sneak out of bed when morning has found us? We pray not. Sinners of a sort. And yet—there you are your nude sleeping form—caught only by the dismal dust of morning—shining forth from your haven porch outside. The forbidden door, always left open. Is it a place to another spring or do I really feel the twilight in the air?

You must have thousands upon thousands of rabbits. Brown baby bunnies furried out there.

They rejoice calmly in the your gifts you grow... for them. And feed them calmly, a carrot from your finger just balanced there. They nibble at the gracious curve of your hand and playfully watch your every move, their ears padding back and forth before your very eyes! They love you Emillio can't you see that?

Chapter Twenty-Nine

God, what a night. The dream, now I know. My God, I must protect Emillio. C-I-v-I-c, but what does that mean? I hurry into my corduroys and ripped green jacket. The fall weather is biting. The city streets are clothed in a cool red, the winter is approaching. I run much and hard faster and faster down to the Bourse Building. Will I make it 'here in time? The sense of urgency is overwhelming. Something tells me this info is in the Curtis Music School. I bang on the door and feverishly try the lock. A kind elderly black gentlemen answers the door for me.

"Excuse me mister...

"Henry." He looks at me with kindly eyes.

"I have a friend who maybe in deep trouble. I had a dream last night in which he won my part. You know we are about to have a war, don't you?" I stand trembling my heart races faster.

"It's ok, what happened?" His voice is soothing.

I stutter, "I, I, I, had a dream where my friend Emillio was being terminated for the war. The letters C-I-v-I-c were the key when I woke."

He replies, "Maybe it stands for civil service."

"Thank you for your time, I must get to him as fast as possible."

I hurriedly press on, as I hop down the steps and begin to rub my eyes I run ever so faster. I fly by the shops and streets. People stare in wonderment, at last the large stately red building looms ahead. I explain the severity of my problem to the desk clerk. He is obliging. Up the elevator. Hurry please. At last the fourth floor, I wind my way through the white tunnel and my heart skips a beat. There is Emillio coming towards me. We exchange quick hellos, his like a razor sharp blade.

He is going to open the door, he grabs me harshly.

"I never want you to come to my office again." He now has me in a bind, my right arm twisted behind me. I shiver. Then, from this contorted position he loosens his grip and we both gaze into each others eyes. He instead paces down the hall. I follow. He bops along like little Lord Fauntleroy. I tag along—he doesn't seem to mind. Outside he glides down the steps. I follow and we get into a cab together. The ride is silent.

"Emillio." The shattering of glass. "I don't want you to go, or to be put in the war we are about to have." No reply. His eyes squint and I notice for the first time the tiny crow's feet edging his eyes in the bright sun.

The car stops. The haircutters—he immediately gets a seat in the chair. I follow him in my torn jacket.

"You see, I had a dream last night that you were going to be recruited for the service." No reply.

"I'm sorry miss", the barber interrupts, "but you can't stay here any longer while this man gets his hair cut."

Chapter Thirty

Pacing and still more pacing. Surely... The radio blurts out, I am not about to die. Sheltered and fed I find the days seem to be intolerable. They push and shove—the good angel occasionally mixing nasty proof with the bad angel. He speaks in hissing tones. Sometimes, she in a tone passionate but inescapable. I look about my window. No, my neighbors are not out in a semi-circle. Perched on their white porch chairs, the way I had envisioned them. They whisper, the voices. "You're very pretty Christina" and his in the wind cries, "She is, but dumb" I write the speech which I have been told to write from the almighty subconscious, how shyness is actually evil. I feel the need to tell all so as preaching is done I sit on my open window on the fourth floor and preach to the night. The lone moon being the only spectator holding its place.

Written during the actual time: Because humans fear rejection—because the devil has led 'them to believe they are no good should constantly be sacrificing more, etcetera, this is wrong. Humans, I feel, should love themselves and shower those they love with love. This is not selfish. However, the devil will delude us to believe it is. It is he who is most quick to judge others jump to conclusions, make one feel badly about ourselves and sacrifice—according to the Bible—should not be used to beat ourselves over the heads like a club. Punishment, but rather sacrifice is beautiful only when used to help others to see the "good." This is love.

That humans should all stand in a perishable line, or parade of sin. According to the Bible, God sent Jesus Christ down to save or to take the burden of all our sins, for he realized that we are sinners and always will be. This does not mean (as the devil might say) that we come back to earth or don't pass through certain spiritual doors. This is untrue. What it does mean is that, if we accept Jesus Christ as our personal savior, then we have no fears because God judges in the end—love and who is one human to judge another? If one has committed suicide in the past—there is no need to sacrifice (in the devil's way) beating one's self over the head that you have to make up, but rather, or if one has killed someone, realize that according to the Bible the only thing you need to know to go to Heaven, is to love yourself and know that God realizes humans are sinners and that is why Jesus Christ was sent down to take the sins away from us and that through our belief in him as our own personal savior we become cleansed and go to Heaven, and become good.

Who is one human to bar the doors to Heaven for another human being? I ask you this. If we succumb to such thinking as we should be better or we should sacrifice, or we shouldn't appreciate our brains or looks or pleasures in life or most of all that we are selfish no matter what. Then that is the devil trying to get us to dislike ourselves. This is not love or God. God gave us gifts and love to appreciate ourselves as well as make others appreciate. If we wish to sacrifice in a Godly way, then we sacrifice perhaps to help others to learn that sacrifice can be positive. Not negative. Sacrifice in God's name, is never used to put ourselves down or others. After all, who is one human being to judge another?

I feel that the problem in the world is a lack of communication that because of shyness people inadvertently become subject to all kinds of evil thoughts. They are afraid of rejection. These come to us in the form of believing others have to be something they are not, blaming people, judging people, and taking things away from other people. When we believe in such things as sacrifice—as punishment i.e. that we should be better than we are, or that others think we should be better than we are, this is destructive thinking. It is the evil. It is a seed which begins to allow people to judge others and torment themselves by such thinking that they will be buried in hell, experimented on—that certain doors on the freeway will be closed to them and better yet, that they are eternally doomed to come back to earth. No human being, I feel can decide for another human being what his or her fate is or will be.

Because people, as humans with weaknesses, are subject to evil thoughts. i.e. it becomes necessary to recognize this, in the light of spirituality. Temptation, the devil—will lead you to believe that he can not only judge our fate and right and wrongs, but the fate of others as well, that we must work our way to heaven's spirituality. No human being I feel, is in the position to judge another human being—for when this is done not only is it selfish but it is obligatory as well.

Sacrifice: Some ways to get rid of evil are to realize his ways of manipulation. These are as follows: judgement through intellectuality. You don't know enough. You should be sacrificing more. Convoluting the Bible into contradictions to help you lose faith. Judging others—

most of all making you judge yourself. This is wrong, please love yourself.

People may say I prognosticate—I am a messenger from God. Even if I wasn't, as long as I am doing good what difference would it make I ask you? The devil has the power to prognosticate. He uses this to delude you into believing that people should be graded rank and file accordingly—how good they are as humans. According to their number spiritually. This is the devil. All human beings are equal. God loves all his children equally. When the devil sees weakness in another, he will jump in and try to convince you that you have some reason to be hurting yourself. Or the only way you are respected as a human, is through telling others what they are. This is wrong. This is evil. When the devil sees you are being good, he slips in and tries to catch you on your downfall.

I feel that the difficulty with men is that because they are able to prognosticate, they try to delude others that women particularly have the power to judge others spiritually—and they are bad because they have to "work," to be good. Or, "work" for their spirituality or "work" to get to Heaven or work to prognostication. Prognostication has absolutely nothing to do with going to Heaven. You do not work to get to Heaven. Just realize Jesus died to save us. God realizes we are sinners and always will be. That is why Christ died for us. No human will ever be Sinless. But our sins do not "bar" us from Heaven. It doesn't even matter how "good" we are. These things are irrelevant as to whether we get to Heaven or not. Don't ever let anyone scare you, that you have to work for your spirituality. The Bible points out that we should be good, only to make it more pleasant for those on Earth. But this has nothing to do with whether or not you go to Heaven.

Chapter Thirty-One

After all; the room stands quiet, the voices have left now. I am no longer guided by my superconscious. I stare out the cold open window, as I watch pedestrians in the hazed orange street glow. A breeze flows through my heart. Stiff they walk not knowing where they are going. All are of God's children so ignorant or has he just deemed me with this special gift. So I am a Christ. Emillio certainly must be the Anti-Christ. I lie down on my mattress on the floor and stare at the dappled ceiling. The light from outside casts shadows of greed through my windows and I Stare upward the night seeming so long. I feel the neon blue cast throughout the room as I sink slowly to slumber.

The next morning I awake 7:05 A.M. God—my body feels wracked with some intangible type of pain. Maybe beings from other planets were injecting me with chemicals all through the night. My head feels mega-cephalic. I do my morning ritual of shower and put on my make—up. Yes; today I look pretty—God must be rewarding me for being so good. Hush—I hear him talk to me above the din… Before going to work today I will make a placard for the back of my jacket: "God Loves You".

I adhere the black magic marker to the white large sheet. I pin it on to my navy coat and walk to work—waving at the cars who I feel are, or prognosticate what they see in me. The walk is long. I know that everyone in Philadelphia knows me. See! That car is turning to see me. He is going my way. This means he must accept Christ. But does he know he is Saved? I smile encouragingly, he nods back. Two more blocks and I will be at the convalescent home. I walk timidly past a construction site. I see the large stone building looming ahead. I press "four," the dining room kitchen floor. A few more paces and I am at the kitchen. I exchange hellos with several of the workers. "What was that you were wearing on your back?" one of the workers asked, his tone awry.

I somewhat embarrassingly hurry up (I know I shouldn't be embarrassed), squash my coat into the metal bin reserved for employees only.

56

Two other girls with long legs and gazelle-type bodies breezed in with a sense of authority.

Do they not like me because I'm white? As we all file into the kitchen and pick up our work tags, I notice one of the employees jokingly waving a knife around. I seriously reprimand him, "Are you not of Christ's body?" Immediately the young man nudged his friend's elbow and both broke into a curious kind of laughter of which I thoroughly disapproved. From the heat of the kitchen to the coziness of the dining room, the three girls and I begin serving the elderly folk. Many gruntles of dislike; "That's not enough," "I want more potatoes," they sing in their harsh tones, one following the other. I reprimand them in a kind way. I actually see each customer as a different sort some seem like vultures, the many years have embittered their souls. The others thankful to be alive, and loving and giving I make a mental data of each. Their age and some ones driftlessness seem so sad. Out of the window the sky is burning a cold red night. Where are they going to go? It seems almost definitely absurd to know, let alone judge, where each will go. Yet, some are smiling, undemanding and nice. Others, no.

I go alone back to the bins and grab my coat, I take the sign off; and try to replenish my mind with better, more welcome thoughts.

Chapter Thirty-Two

I change into my yellow sleeper. The sun has just broke in through my window and the sun feels like a friend that I never really knew but is oh so caring. On my palette I mix all the colors. I turn on the radio and listen. Yes, they still are talking about me, the different stages I am going through. You see, Emillio paid each station manager to play songs to help build my level of intelligence up to his level. You see, as one matures commensurately, so ones level of intelligence goes up. As I know it is a gift from God and faith is all that is needed.

The radio blurts out that there was a plane crash with two Americans onboard. I drop my brush and change into my jeans. I pull on quickly my shirt, the door slams and I run to Emillio's apartment. No, no, he's not at home. My God, maybe he's been killed. No, this can't be. My eyes begin to water as I look at the car parked in front of his apartment. I see in the front seat a filled Hefty bag, some joke. Is this a sign? Was Emillio really killed? I run breathlessly to the nearest pay phone, and my sister answers. She doesn't understand. The call is such that I break out in tears. Someone, please understand. Two young men stop to listen to my story—but I feel more morbid curiosity than anything else. And then they are gone. I spend the rest of my day moping through the city streets, my swollen eyes and red face known only to me. How could God take him from me? I wander in and out of shops and go to the bus station— all cold glances. Am I being punished? I explain my story to a man there and he confirms my story. He said, "Some things happen that way." I spend the rest of my evening crying harder than I ever had before.

A week later, as I walk through Rittenhouse Square my body is still weak and my being torn with pain. I see a man. My God he walks like Emillio. No it couldn't be. It is! His head turns slightly, "My God I thought you were dead." "You see there was a plane crash and I thought you were onboard."

A slight tilt of the head and an odd expression hastens me on my way. I promise I won't get wrapped up in my intelligence ever again.

Chapter Thirty-Three

The next day I awake and go to the laundromat. But why are these cars making gestures as to guns are at their heads. They must all hate me. Someone is going to kill me. Maybe it is a warning. Maybe it is Emillio's plan. I run to my apartment. My God, what am I going to do? These people want me dead for some reason. I will have to stay in my apartment all day. I run from the laundromat to my apartment. As I bolt the door I realize my phone has been turned off for nearly six months now. I hide under my Parsons table. But what's this? Everyone is honking. Are they angry? The voices say they are—no it's a wedding. Emillio must have gotten married. God no! No! No! No! I cry as hard as I've ever cried in my life (it must be the writer, the girl with the dog). I am crying now but I begin to vomit. I feel that a metal pipe has been thrust from ear to ear. I stumble out of my flat and the light is so bright. I trip up Emillio's apartment and ring his bell. I push through his outside door. I stumble up the stairs. I rap on the apartment above his. A kind young girl invites me in. I explain my story. She loans me towels as I vomit over her toilet. I stay about two hours. "Thank, you so much, you are most kind." "But do…" "You…" "Know if he was married?" No reply.

There are fewer cars outside my apartment now. I go home and stay up for hours contemplating. All I can think of is how much I want to die.

Chapter Thirty-Four

It is Fall now and I have not seen Emillio for months. Wearing my painted overalls and torn green battle jacket, I haunt my usual territory—Rittenhouse Square. I have no money left today but I must have a joint. I bring small objects from my apartment to bargain with. A young black man sits relaxed on the far bench wearing a black leather jacket. We make the deal inconspicuously. I carry home with me this precious jewel. When the door shuts behind me I light up. Coughing between each smoke—soon the painting I had started takes on a whole new sort of way. I paint mixing this color with blue and the whole process seems never ending and the enjoyment immense.

As evening clouds in I will sneak up the street to see Emillio. I don my full—length medieval leather jacket and ruffled white shirt. He invites me in. We speak lazily to each other for a few moments and then he ushers me to the door.

Chapter Thirty-Five

Sitting inside my apartment I sit cross—legged and watch the day turn to her marveling gowns of pink through the window. Her ever—changing, I see the clouds—God's glory splattered across the night defining her territory. I can feel Emillio in my mind. It's been one year maybe he is dead. I stare at the colors. Questioning tears well up inside. Staring, yet I can feel home. I dream of a world, no one else would know. And we become two spirits carried off in the night in her steely cold.

> In Your Own
> An anguish.
> The death…
> Two spirits leave for another universe
> Sterilized
> Synchronized
> Metal feet tap loudly to the silent beat.

We fly together. Outside there are cars traveling everywhere and nowhere. He has come to my apartment, but once. So long ago. As we entered the door we took quiet steps and lay down next to each other. A peaceful being. We fed on the love exuded there. And he looked at my paintings in awe. But that was the end of that though we remained virginal in body. In my mind. He walked in my bathroom and seemed to disappear. Where he lovingly placed his bugging device there for me, yet we have a connection. I can usually see him as I do now in my mind's eye coming out of his apartment. Jarred to reality I wipe the tears with my bare arm and run up to his apartment. There he is coming down the stairs. A half smile becoming his angelic face. He breezes by, into a cab—the words I long to say, come out as tears. God how I love you Emilio. Will I ever see you again?

Chapter Thirty-Six

The days are getting shorter. The miraculous trees that are towering above my apartment. The branches reach to the windows in hues of startling yellow, red and green. Almost neon-electric. I sit on my chair lost in thought. I am jarred by my doorbell's ring. I am not expecting anyone. I put some pants over my dirtied yellow frock, I lightly traipse down the carpeted stairs and see to my surprise my mother and sister— she seems stiff and frozen. We feel a whoosh of warm air as I shut the door and let them in.

"We would like to know", my mother starts, in hushed tones, "if you would like to go for a drive in the country?" her face framed in plastic, her last word sounding somewhat frightened.

I wonder why this came up so suddenly. There is an aura of strangeness about the whole thing. My mother has only come down to my apartment twice in this past year. However, I am overjoyed that they have asked me. I accept. With an uncertainty that cannot be defined.

The three of us wander out into the cool heat of the day. My sister's blond curly hair shining like a halo below the sun. The car doors slam, driving with my mother and speaking with her, I realize we are exactly on the same spiritual plane. Our intelligence is present and the same. However, something is bothering her. The conversation between the three of us is stilted. The sky a beautiful blue, and white Clouds, like the foam of the ocean, seems to pour into the sky. My mother is gripping the wheel and looks forward so directly at the road. My questions are attended to inadvertently. A rare glance from the driver. Something inside me tells me something is wrong as we round beautiful trees and wondrous sights, neither seems to care. As we round a bend I realize that we are actually following a destiny. The grey cement building hovers above the grass. No! This can't be. A nasty voice inside hisses out: Norristown State Mental Institution.

Suddenly the car is filled with screams. They're coming from everywhere. I'm wrapped up on my sister's lap. As the police officer walks strictly towards the car I am found screaming: "No! No! No!" and pulling every hair out of my sister's head. She clutches me the door still open. I accidently push on my mother's foot on top of the accelerator. The car careens, the door open and we nearly hit a tree. Then I escape, my mother yells to a soldier that just happens to be standing by—"Grab her!" I am fighting with all my passion. Someone is hysterical. The screams seem to come from beyond. As the hysterics continue, I become lost in delirium. As I am told inside: "You have to stay here for five days". It rings in my ears. Building 16. 1 am jostled into a bare room. A young woman in a sari greets me sternly. At this point I feel that I must show that I am normal. My mother and sister stand in another room and I give them unforgiving looks. They are standing looking so Sad. I harshly bark out: "I will never forgive you for this." As I stamp this on their foreheads. They leave.

I sit down with the young doctor. She asks me a series of questions. I try—to answer as normally as possible. But I am normal. My mother leaves. My sister leaves. I sit rigid in the chair, as her probing eyes pass over me. She seems so cold.

I am ushered back into a room, a magazine in the room. I lie still on the bed. One false move of my body and I won't make it out in five days. I lie on my bed and pretend to read. "Christina," a young chubby woman interrupts. "Will you please come with me?" I follow.

Sitting on top of the doctors table my reflexes are tested, the room a bright canary yellow. I josh with the doctor and nurse. While an inner wall of turmoil presents itself and draws nigh. With perseverance I press on. The two seem quite understanding. I change into a hospital gown. I spend the rest of the day, lying on my bed watching the room grow darker and darker. I hear voices from other rooms. No, I will not let them know my secret of the things present in my mind. I know, however, that they can somehow read it. And I can somehow read theirs. We keep this spirit present.

The next day I wander out and down the hallway. Somehow I feel a sickly spiritual feeling. I realize that the good and evil are fighting for dominancy in my head. The thing to do pray and preach. I know of course, that I may possibly be one of the second Christ's. You see, I felt at the time as though each world, each millisecond in time, on each and every habitable planet like earth of the universe, each has a Christ. Some people make it spiritually to this point—others not, but not until you reach this point—from coming back, life after life do you finally reach heaven. I sit on the bench and stare at the painted rainbow on the wall. Each color so significant of the different stages which must be reached before death. I sit and stare trying to ignore the sickly feelings. I ask the nurse if she will lend me a Bible to preach with. They do not have one. A few minutes later, my doctor comes to see me. They are injecting me with Haladol. Suddenly seconds later, I experience the most horrifyingly hellish feeling my body has ever known. That my arms and legs should be cut off. That my soul is confined and trapped within my body. My God!!! I can't handle this! I want to die. My God I want to die. "But Christina, if you die you will be giving up all God has given you." says a shallow female voice. Yes, but I love you God I don't want to hurt you. I love myself, but this torture is unbearable. I now sit up against the wall my arms crossed behind my back; someone asks me what I am doing. "Nurse, nurse—I can't... take this anymore." The nurse with a speculative glance surmises I need more. "My God I've got to make a call. I have twenty cents."

"Hello Laura—I feel," getting the words out is excruciatingly painful, "I feel suicidal", my voice shaking.

"Click".

I begin to cry hysterically. I have one dime left, I shakingly work this mechanical wondermind.

"Laura— I am suicidal, I, I, I, I can't take this anymore."

She hangs up.

I furtively go to my room where I find my blue bathrobe – I take the tie out and hide it under my gown. I open the door to the ladies room, using the metal triangular hinge above the door I fasten the noose; I climb on top of the metal trash can, put, my head in the noose and kick the can away. The first feeling I have as I am dangling above is forgiveness. "Oh Lord, please forgive me." However, I can feel two spirits present. Two evil spirits. In pale whitish pink and blue. I cannot actually see them, but they seem to be in control of the hanging. I feel the blood rushing out of my face. Each breath is now shorter and shorter. The room begins to fade. I believe a few minutes later I feel the door opening.

"Oh! My God!" She stares and leaves to get...

Soon the room is filled with—several people. They are cutting me down. I numbly follow her orders. I feel hazy and light. I follow the doctor to a small booth where I am asked a series of questions.

"Your intelligence seems to be intact," claims the modest doctor in relief.

"But Dr. Epstein didn't I suffer brain damage I... can feel it."

He stretches back in his seat eying me. "No."

The hanging itself was gruesome—but now I am—approached by yet another.

"Will you come with us please. Christina?"

I follow through the cold cement walls and uncarpeted halls—up a flight of steps by two attendants dressed crisply their faces worn and ravaged. I am led into a large comfortable room where a long large mahogany table separates the five gentlemen from each other. I am asked to sit at the head opposing the main man dressed in a comfortable business suit. Startled as I turn around I see my mother and two sisters wearing feigned expressions of grief and pity. This can only hurt me more—Make them go away. I can't understand, what is this all about?

"Christina, you tried suicide by hanging. Is this true or untrue?"

I nod; feeling sick to my stomach. The man with the low resonant voice asks me again, "What made you try to do this?"

"Well." I feel choked up. "Two evil spirits told me to." The last word hangs in the air.

Many more questions. It seems these men are enjoying themselves. I am briskly ushered out. Are they letting me free? The hope is dashed by a wired up window on a nearby van. I am transported to the van. Where am I going someone please tell me where I am going!

After what seems like an eternity the van pulls up to this finely done building with more plants and a gravel drive. I am led inside and introduced. Some of the nurses seem quite pleasant, others somewhat mean. I cling to my bag of belongings. I am shown into a room where my supposed roommate is sitting like a statue in a chair in a corner of the room dressed in black. The nurse explained that she is a little disturbed. She frightens me with her hostile expression. That night I am given sleeping pills to get to sleep.

As the light hazily filters through the brightly patterned window curtains, I find it difficult to get up. A nurse yells up and down the hall knocking on each door to make sure that the patients are awake. It seems so highly technical.

Morning meeting begins and I am confronted by twenty or so patients. A barrage of questions are discussed and many patients stare at me like an anomaly. After group, several strangers introduce themselves. The tv is put on. One of the doctors asks me into an office he seems kind. I sit on the chair as one would sit on the edge of rocks far out to sea. Very carefully. He asks me a standard outline of questions for new patients but somehow he represents the judgement in purgatory or maybe he is! I react strongly. As he probes and makes me feel more guilty about my suicide and the ensuing slaughter which I will go through because of it. I react violently. I thrash and yell at him. It wasn't my fault, I had a common adverse reaction to Halodol. A feeling of suicide. But what or who he represents I'll never know. I try to explain to him that I am the second Christ. But how could I be with the attempt? I am so confused, my identity loses itself I storm out of the office. Two nurses get to me.

"Here are your morning pills."

"No! No! I won't take any pills."

"What about the vitamins?" The nurse firm in her direction.

"No!"

I go back to my room. Almost instantly the nurse comes over.

"No Christina you must stay out in the day room."

"But I'm not going to try anything." The tears blind my speech and something is caught in my throat. All I want to do is sleep.

As evening draws near the t.v. great Sony god blaring out evil, such a horror—unpeaceful messages.

"Christina Alexanda was found today shot outside her apartment," says the newscaster.

I knew they weren't on my side—I knew people were trying to kill me. That girl... I know she represents me. God I hope they don't find me here.

"...And now a commercial for Eveready Batteries."

"Energize me."

A commercial in evil advertising. Why would anyone want to try to kill themselves? I feel fatigue setting in, yet I feel so overstimulated. I turn into my room. 3 A.M. I am awakened by a bitter smell that permeates my every pore. A smell of death. Another patient down the hall lets out a series of anguished screams. I know they are trying to poison us. I stumble over to the nurses station.

"No Christina we don't smell anything.

I go back to sleep. Beginning to consider my two suicide attempts I call Emilio. After three rings, a groggy hello. My voice shaking, "Emilio, have you ever tried suicide?" A final click and he hangs up on me just the way he used to when I lived in my apartment.

The next morning the patients are all lined up to go somewhere. Are they going to be put in ovens and killed? I am not supposed to go with them. Will my turn come up soon? I begin to tremble. Maybe more faith in Christ? I open the lid to my breakfast tray and the food seems repulsive, especially the pork. I put the lid back on. Sacrifice I must sacrifice.

Three days go by without eating. The nurses prod me to eat. I won't. I must look for spiritual endurance. I ask the head nurse for a bible. She hands me one called "The Way". That evening after everyone has fallen into the land of deep sleep I read "The Way". Pictures at the head of each chapter of people starving, people on bloody war grounds, my God!! Is this what's going to happen to me after I die? I know I nearly killed myself and showed a lack of appreciation, but, is this really me?

That evening I stay up as late as possible reading the Bible. Why all these sacrifices? For the next few days, I cannot be torn from the Bible finally one of the malevolent nurses says to me in a singsong voice, "If you don't put that Bible away I'll put you in the confinement room" I explain to her that it is necessary to preach to the other patients so she uncaringly put me in the confinement room for three hours or so. Inside this white electric box I can hear the football game on the outside. They are counting off spiritual misdemeanors. My spiritual misdemeanors. I realize the only way to escape them is to astrally project. I try to project by first rendering my body (material) useless. I realize if I don't get out of my body now, then I will go to hell when I die. I start taking breaths. Holding longer and longer. A total relief sweeps over the torture I have endured when I hear the keys of the nurse at the door.

As the sky outside grows dark I am stung with the horrible sensation of what is going to happen to me when I die. Revelations—and hornet—like creatures stinging people in so much pain they want to die. This can't be! Could it really be the table of elders playing games with we Earthlings'? Actually, Revelations seems more like a love between Jezebel and He who created the earth. I smell that odor again, is it a warning? I fear myself. Scary as it may seem to devote to reading the entire Bible. As I go to bed I think maybe when you die you become two selves. Both materialistic. And one self sits in a chair and watches on a screen what the first self has gone through in life on Earth and made to go through all the pain and torture again by being strapped to a chair with monitors to transfer the feelings to the other body.

Chapter Thirty-Seven

"Christina, Christina! Christina wake up!" A jolt as my eyes open as if their first to the world. Yes, my roommate is lying on her bed collapsed in clothes upon clothes. Watching her figure in repose I witness the face a mask completely devoid of expression.

I feel a prick in my arm as some liquid is slowly injected into my vein. "She only slept two hours." "Yes I know," said sympathetically one nurse to another. I see two strange men enter the room with a tall long white metal table. The thing scares me. I am told to "just roll over" on to it. I feel the weakness of my body. I am strapped down. Covered with a white blanket. The two men wheel me outside. Where am I going? I know not. Am I going to be killed! A sweep of fear, then quick relief, in my wanting to abstain from such belief. The trip in the ambulance takes ages. I'm sure that the other people outside know it's me and where I'm going. My thoughts race on. Maybe they are going to take me—and then the sharp intonation of the driver, "We are taking you to Jefferson Hospital." I find this so upsetting. I don't need to be hospitalized! My eyes by now are growing very tired. My arms are limp. Past a glass booth with several people inside I am unstrapped and put in a room with four cement white walls. I wait for hours. There's a Newsweek magazine. I will just read this now. To prove to all who are reading my mind that I'm not dumb. I hear the honks of horns outside goading me on. But these letters and words? I can't put them together or make sense of it—it must be because of my suicide attempt. I must be a vegetable. With horror I try to scream, but I—am mute. I will try to kill myself, but how? I frantically search the empty room the windows' metal grating. Instead I take to breaking my fingers on the floor. I pushed down so hard that the knuckles turned white. They will not break. I try harder, soon… enough, a nurse comes in, looks at what I'm doing, but does nothing. I am reduced to tears and choking on my saliva. I am all alone. Won't somebody help me!

Soon I am strapped in a bed. My passively letting them manhandle me, the bright neon light up above stares down at me the way God would look unfavorably out at a fool. My legs are strapped each one, my body, then each arm. As the nurses, etc. talk, I can see it is about Heaven and Hell and who, they argue, is on a higher spiritual level, and how I am going to Hell. They come and they go—each treating me as a dog begging for nourishment. It has long gone without. Please release these arms. This leg. Please. No tender hand to caress my brow. Only sharp stinging glares and loud voices. I must do something now. I must die to prove to them I am the second Christ. Am I? If I don't, then I will surely come back to Earth in a horrible form. I force my arms up against the leather shackles with all I have. I continue this for so long that it is getting too late. Oh this pain, this torture. Maybe if I bite off my tongue—yes after chewing a great deal on the bloody mass it becomes almost severed in two.

Soon a tall distinguished doctor breezes in. The nurses gather round; like some sacrifice they speak in muddied tones. Their language indiscernible. I see a large needle as I am injected in the arm. Soon, as they dissipate I feel the room slowly darken, and voices of all the spiritual combat recede and blur away into nothing.

The next morning when I am roused by a nurse I see a little paper cup of water and a cup of pills. The orange juice—like substance is clean going down, the pills harder still. I look the nurse—directly in the eye. There is nothing there. As she leaves – I happen to catch a glimpse of the woman in the bed next to me. She is sleeping soundly. All I want to do is sleep. I don't know why, but I feel that is all I want to do. The horns are still honking outside. I try to plug my ears, I want to scream. I groggily creep out of bed to the bathroom where I find two pieces of toilet paper. I roll them into small balls, then wet them. I force them in my ears and curse the demons putting me through this hell. I twist and turn beneath the covers. I am startled, I hear two raps on the door, the doctor I saw before greets me in his stern manner.

"Hello Christina, my name is Dr. Henderson. How are you?"

I return, "I feel alright thank you". Believing I will be punished if I don't say I'm fine.

He asks, "What did you have for breakfast today?"

"I didn't have breakfast."

After he leaves, I try to vomit the pills up. I retch and I retch. I am in a MENTAL INSTITUTION; the words bang on my brain like steel drums though somehow discordant. I'm not sick!

Two weeks later I have lost fifteen pounds and am now very skinny. Each day consists of trying desperately to sleep—because all I want to do is die. But my roommate hates me. I've asked her on two occasions to shut the door when she leaves. It is an excess of stimuli. But also she will not stop her smoking in bed upon her request. She slides into the bedroom on vinyl slippers and hisses at me saying very strange things in angry tones. At one point, she tries to provoke me into getting physical with her. I escape to the next room. The t.v. is talking about Heaven and Hell spiritually too. But because I can't understand it, I realize I am surely a vegetable. Then my roommate walks in. I go out as soon as possible. I make a phone call to Emilio. One ring, two rings. A soft female voice answers, "Hello".

"Yes, may I speak with Emilio please?"

"He isn't here at the moment", her voice smooth and kind.

"Well I just called to say I love him."

"I love him too."

"You mean", I hesitate, "that you're engaged to him?"

"Yes."

"Thank you", my voice slowly ripening into tears.

Today I am being forced to go to group—because I refuse to go to any groups, I have been trying to spit up my pills, and have been so depressed I can't even get myself out of bed, the doctor asks me if I am suicidal. I say no. Lying. I know I will be punished by this lie but being on this unit is killing me.

I go to art therapy. We draw a picture of how we feel. I draw a stick, figure. The art therapist cannot stand me, that is obvious. When my turn comes around I say, close to tears, "I am afraid of going to Hell because I tried suicide". Suddenly every member of the group says, "Yes you will go to Hell it's in the Bible". I am so frightened I can't even cry. Pictures of torture and torment fill my brain like the currents of the Sea. One endlessly following another.

More weeks go by. More pills and more therapy which consists of simple dialogue with my doctor of what I had to eat that day.

One day, as the voices that were killing me as well as every little noise, disappear. My doctor explains to me in Laymans terms what I have. I don't know how to react.

I still remember though all the meanings, symbolisms and significance of what I had been through spiritually has been branded on my brain leaving scars never to heal. I know it will never go away but who knows what is real.

Chapter Thirty-Eight

After slowly recovering over two years from the memories, severe depression, sleeping each day from 4 P.M. to 8 P.M. and limiting agoraphobia, I remembered the name of a doctor I once went to during my illness in the—city. A Dr. Higgans. I remembered him as the kind fatherly type. I decided it was about time for therapy so I set up an appointment. When I arrived at his plush office he was congenial and very nice—though he kept alluding that I was going to have a breakdown. Now I felt fine, but came to see him basically because of my "attacks" which speculatively were defined as psychosis, but may be due to epilepsy as an EEG revealed (I had been in and out of various hospitals during these two years with this undefinable Hell). They are the most hellish things to go through. No one can even imagine or know what they are like. They can be seen in outward appearance as innocuous but what one goes through in the mind is the crux of it. A terrifying loss of control of ones' mind (endangering oneself but not others).

Dr. Higgans prescribed Inipramine for my agoraphobia which I took faithfully. After ten days on it I developed some strange feelings. Inability to sleep, hypersensitivity to name but a few of the nine symptoms I was experiencing. I began to grow terribly anxious and asked him what I should do. One time I called him up, he would reply, "Take more Inipramine, take more Inipramine". Like a broken thought swelling in my mind in this lost state. Then the night came. I broke into a full psychosis. My sister rushed me to the hospital. We waited for hours sitting, me pacing in the emergency ward. Wanting to sleep but being unable in this glass cage. Since there was no room we rushed to a private institution. We speeded along through the pitch black night. My sister told them that in the PDR it says under allergies to Inipramine: psychosis. I had practically all the symptoms. I was taken off the Inipramine (the doctor apparently had been prescribing an abnormal amount as well as all the other drugs I was on). I was there for a good four weeks. When I got out, I was ok for a couple of weeks then broke through again. I would go to sleep at night and hear people scream in terror being tortured "don't do that no, no, no!". The radio emitted sounds sounding like Russian and German. I went back to PPC. As my eyes revolved around the room I could feel an attack coming on. My eyes got fixated on everything, making visual patterns out of anything and everything and voices began to sound like they were referring to me and spirituality negatively. It was as if the voices were competing to see who was good and who was evil. Although much more complicated then that. Mostly that we all are, going to go to Hell. If you were good you were alright. If bad—you preyed on peoples' selfishness. One had to keep perfectly still physically so as not to noisily acknowledge any evil statement. One acknowledgement to the bad, or one wrong word, or shift of clothing or body or a sound would be accompanied by hellish thoughts and pictures of neon abstracts in the head and of persecution. The voices and noises heard, all fit together like a spiritual puzzle. I was put in a little room adjoining the nurses station to make sure I would be alright. I had been up 34 hours with this and being in that location only exacerbated my problem because of excess stimuli. The room consists of a bare mattress on the floor. I was so suicidal I can't even begin to tell how. As all their voices were coming at me I desperately asked the nurse to use the pay phone. We got there and I began to tell everything to my mother in broken sobs. I realized how much she meant to me all in one big rush. I became hysterical. "You don't know what this is like." The terror, the tears stream down my face as I screamed, "I want to die I WANT TO DIE". Suddenly I hear the phone drop heavily onto the floor, "hello mom— mom!". I feel sick all of a sudden. What if? My sister got on the phone, "Christina mom's fainted", she said in a scared way. Then she hung up. I started to wildly speculate: what if she had a heart attack? I walk back to the bare room tracing each pattern on the carpet. Stiff and cold I huddled. I clasp my knees tightly together and for the first time in my life, really prayed. Dear God please let my mother go to Heaven and Michael (my boyfriend) and Joyann (my sister). I also prayed for my release from this psychosis. I could feel for the first time in my life what a truly unselfish prayer was. Within seconds I saw a huge bright light in my mind's eye. I felt a rush go from my feet to my head and within seconds the voices all died down to nothing. A miracle. I come out of the psychosis within minutes. And what I thought to myself was "The lion lies down with the lamb". It was the first time in my life after being up with the hellish psychosis that I had my prayers answered. I was

stunned'. My sister phoned me and let me know that mom was al
Since then I have truly felt the power of God. For I had been giv
drugs. It was an epiphany.

Chapter Thirty-Nine

After being out of the hospital for a few weeks, the drug which I had been prescribed, broke through. Beginning with a feeling of ill at ease—it intensifies to the point of longing to die. My whole world collapses around me. I had been hoping and praying that this would be the drug that would "cure" me of my anxiety attacks. But as I lay in my bed at night at home I could feel the hundreds of bugs crawling all over my body. The people talk to me in sinister voices—all different languages. Their hissing thoughts spewing out like sewage on a city pavement. The broken scream of a tortured man. I try to cover my head with my pillow but they are in my head. Soon I can't take it any longer—I scream from the top of my lungs. My mother quietly opens the bedroom door. Pain is written all over her face. She quietly sits down and in the dark room, the only light streams through the door silhouetting her face and her beautiful fine features. The tears slide down my face. "I DON'T WANT TO LIVE ANYMORE MUM, I WANT TO DIE—I CANT TAKE IT ANYMORE!" The dialogue becoming more perverse with each breath. My mother's hand caresses my forehead.

The emergency ward is extremely busy for 2:00 in the morning. By 6:00 A.M. I stand pacing the floor ritualistically thinking and alternately praying for it a to end. We are told to go to another hospital. The car speeds along the night drive. Suicidal thoughts piercing holes in my brain. We wait and wait. The same scenario which usually presents us. My mother and sister are patient. So patient. Finally I am shown a room. They leave. I lay in bed—my hands clasped in prayer. "Please God—let this end, please God—let this end." Over and over.

Thirty hours with no sleep. I squirm around in my bed finding no solace. The attack is unending. (I am still disoriented. A doctor comes in and shoots several questions at me. I don't even know what I am saying, because when I have attacks I become afraid to speak for fear the devil will try to hurt me.) Then a new doctor. He is so kind and gentle. The nicest doctor I have ever had. Then—a new drug. (I have been taken off all my old drugs for about a week.) Within days I am breaking out in a rash. So many questions. Do we try a different drug? This one or that, a new drug is tried. After four weeks no bad symptoms have shown. Yet I realize, if this is the real drug—I will never know, because I could breakout again—and can't lead a "normal" life. It is all a matter of time.

Today we have cooking class. As we enter the bowels of the building my eyes catch the most pathetic sight that I have ever seen in my life. I feel a sickening knife through my heart. Other patients stare at him and speak in audible tones about this poor person. I become irate. His body had been burned all over, beyond recognition. A horrifying sight. I feel like crying. Instead, I find myself drawn to him. I smile at him, we have a brief chat. He seems touched. My heart goes out to him and I am left wanting to help him more but being unable too. At least I met up to talk to him. All he needed was just a little bit of love. Although he said the firebomb was not meant for him he said he was "glad it happened to him" because he knew he "was the only one who could handle it".

Chapter Forty

Rubbing my eyes the morning sun caresses my face. I feel a little better on my new medication. But this is a stunted, stilted I life—existence. Me and my mind of play—dough, to act on the merest flight of fancy of a drug. Prolixinn and Lithium, in this way.

My doctor and mother have been hoping for me to get a job.

Why is this sock not going on? My foot is clumsy and large. Painstakingly I force the wool—cotton, polyester, mass on. Noticing the fine hairs on my leg. Another day has begun. Stumbling on to my feet—I greet the morning. Yes there are all those years of waking up in my mother's house seeing the light of day, in agony. Hours stretching ahead. Unable to place myself. The momentous proportions of youth. A whole life ahead of me, of what? Hell? I glance easily at the grub of fat wrapped—tight around my body. I was once beautiful. Like a poor, retarded person. I spend my days going for walks with my mother. Always in the way. I am a burden. Defunct, Useless.

I am ready to work now. It's been ten years of living hell—with an occasional glimpse of light through an institution window. I have been admitted over thirteen times in ten years.

"God, please help me find a babysitting job for a doctor's family. One that I can walk to and that pays a lot of money, babysitting for children over two years of age." My hands tightly fastened to one another. Amen. For, that's all I am able to do.

Then looking through the paper—an ad catches my eye. The interview. Trying to impress. Functioning at low level. The words coming out muddied. Pulling at my pathetic, hand made portfolio of paintings done during manic highs, out of my pocket. Fumbling. I slowly begin to realize that not only are these two nice parents doctors! But they live right around the corner and are willing to pay me handsomely for my work!

It's been two years now, working for the Halls. The grandfather clock tics heavily in the sparsely decorated living room. All is quiet now. I slowly change the dial on my radio and hear a preacher. He is talking about Christianity. I have always felt drawn to religion but I have never heard of "born—again." Fumbling, I write down the phone number on a piece of scrap paper.

And on the phone with Reverend Turner.

"What is born—again?"

John 1:12,13: "12 Yet to all who received him, to those who believed in his name, he gave the right to become children of God—13 children born not of natural descent, nor of human decision or a husband's will, but born of God." (NIV)

The Bible, I was always afraid to peek at it. Look at it. But I have always wanted to. This is exciting!

The preacher resounds. "You must be born again." John 3:36: "36 Whoever believes in the Son has eternal life, but whoever rejects the Son will not see life, for God's wrath remains on him." (NIV) John 5:24: "24 I tell you the truth, whoever hears my word and believes him who sent me has eternal life and will not be condemned; he has crossed over from death to life." (NIV) and again

John 6: 37: "37 All that the Father gives me will come to me, and whoever comes to me I will never drive away." (NIV).

John 6:47: "47 I tell you the truth, he who believes has everlasting life." (NIV)

John 8:31-32: "31 To the Jews who had believed him, Jesus said, 'If you hold to my teaching, you are really my disciples. 32 Then you will know the truth, and the truth will set you free." (NIV).

John 8:36: "36 So if the Son sets you free, you will be free indeed." (NIV)

John 10:28-30: "28 I give them eternal life, and they shall never perish; no one can snatch them out of my hand. 29 My Father, who has given them to me, is greater than all; no one can snatch them out of my Father's hand. 30 1 and the Father are one." (NIV)

John 20:31: "31 But these are written that you may believe that Jesus is the Christ, the Son of God, and that by believing you may have life in his name." (NIV).

John 3:16-21: "16 For God so loved the world that He gave his one and only Son, that whoever believes in him shall not perish but have eternal life. 17 For God did not send his Son into the world to condemn the world, but to save the world through him. 18 Whoever believes in him is not condemned, but whoever does not believe stands condemned already because he has not believed in the name of God's one and only Son. 19. This is the verdict: Light has come into the world, but men loved darkness instead of light because their deeds were evil. 20 Everyone who does evil hates the light, and will not come into the light for fear that his deeds will be exposed. 21 But whoever lives by the truth comes into the light, so that it may be seen plainly that what he has done has been done through God." (NIV)

It's the knowing for sure broadcast. "Christina, you can come to Jesus Christ personally right now. Pray with me, and mean it with your whole heart. "Lord Jesus ... I confess that I am not good ... I have sinned a great deal .... I cannot save myself .... Please forgive me and come into my life ... give me the free gift of eternal life .... and send the Holy Spirit to live in me and help me live for you."

I feel a slight high afterward, a filling of the head. Floating almost in my mind. A numbness and a seriously beautiful one.

It was here that my whole life began to change.

Chapter Forty-One

Hazy, lazy days give birth to moments alone on my bed. Crickets call outside. An occasional shower—it gives relief from the heat that stifles me.

I rest now. Spread naked on my bed. Days march on through my head—as I realize. Wait, it must be time to take my pills. Well, I will just rest now—a little longer.

My head swells and undulates—as—dim light peeps through my half-open shade laying in patterned stripes on the wall. Hmm. It must be morning. My eyes float downward. Clutching a glass, I take my pills. One perphenazine, lithium. This must be the morning, or the evening? I take one more of these, swelling under my breath and gulp down the appropriate amount.

The days drift on. Waking. Occasionally, I guess the amount of my pills. Rarely I wake. It's a binding of a sheet, wrapped tightly around me in sleep, holding me close like the comforting grip of the Land of Nod. I do not have any knowledge what day it is what time. Or what I am taking.

Dizzily I confront and awaken to the sound of a man's voice. Justin. Echoing through the hall-way. In my haste I sit perched on the edge of my bed, like some clown like parrot, only to see him appear, like a vapor. My, I try looking at him.—Words are caught in the ferris—wheel above, in my brain. "Christina" Destructive—torn words issue forth from my lips. I try to smile. Their sound is really concerning me. I know something is wrong; however I feel absolute lack of fear. Justin is concerned.

Upon standing, my two bent pipe-like wobbly legs confess to me as my dizzying brain screams and I lurch forward, these two legs collapse. I crawl on the floor? I can't stand up! Why?

He sees, something is amiss. Upon this awareness, Justin collects himself and cleans in tattered pieces the excrement lying on the floor. Expelled from my mass of body trying to maneuver my way to the bathroom, like some blood-shot animal. With no protection and seeking cover. He is upset. Slowly gathering my bright floral KMart shirt and matching shorts, and knobby white shoes.

My hand. A quick fall into a drinking glass and he is telling me that "We are going to the hospital or we're—breaking up." No fear. Where am I? He operates the faucet as I watch water stream into the bathtub. Pearly drops tumbling down, concentrating on trying not to fall forward and drown, or backward and drown, I steady my nude form. I cleanse myself with great difficulty. The figure in the doorway appears again with my clothes as I dress.

A ride to the hospital. I left half of my memory back there. In the stair—well, gripping tightly to Justin's arm;—to the brown, dark wooden handrail. Out into the sudden, blinding white summers day. Upon question upon question. The reverberating psychedelic rubber balls, of words—alarm and agitate in their friction—the (nurse?) woman questioning me. I pass out. Wheeled into a nearby room. Tubes in place. I am rushed to I.C.U. I die a thousand deaths. Invisibly. I left half of my memory back there. Diagnosis: Pneumonia with extreme dehydration, and, Lithium Toxicity.

A binding of white tape wrapped around and around my body I pull it off, like some circus snake. Blood drips down.

Velvet eyes fluttered with lashes slowly open. A deer, as if to gaze upon the first sight of her new-born fawn. A smile has been playing calmly, mysteriously upon my lips since I can remember. Why? I waken. The walls are off white. I am in the hospital. I have no fear, no wonder, no panic. No questions. I feel a surprising great…deep, undisturbed peace, as if I were at, the most comfortable place I have been—home.

I greet the hospital staff and personnel, the doctors, etc. Everything's going to be okay.

Upon trying to stand, I realize that I no longer have the use of my legs. Only sole, inaudible, indiscernible speech is directed to others. Like chewing on garbage. I sound like a mouthful of precious marbles, through a smile. Colors colliding. I imitate as mouth positions and mimicking sounds I try to direct to her. She is kind. Soon I am to realize that the speech therapist (who has only seen me a few times), says, my recovery is "remarkable," and that I don't need her any longer.

Day and night, I spend blissfully witnessing to everyone in the hospital. Not as a forced prerequisite but as a seemingly eternal Joy. Peace. Everyone. I am happy. I am in fellowship with the Lord. I have been praying, "Thy will be done." (The bitter corner of the chocolate bar eludes me not.) God is good. "Thy will be done."

Upon returning home, the use of my legs is coming back!! The quietness of an early spring. Yes! and a crocus peeping pastels through the earth.

Praise the Lord: I can walk again. I can talk again, as if nothing had happened at all.

(I had no damage from the lithium toxicity or the other drugs and my condition).

My doctor who followed me, said he couldn't attribute my complete recovery to anything other than that it was a miracle, healed through my faith in Jesus Christ.

Praise the Lord, my God and my All.

Amen.

Afterword

Schizophrenia and Christian Life

Life with schizophrenia was torture before therapy and " born–again" Christianity (which I consider the key to my well being). Life before I became a Christian was chaotic, reckless, meaningless, hopeless, fruitless, and laden with pain, sorrow, discord, and abandonment.

Life as a born–again Christian is joyful, meaningful, orderly, harmonious, abundant, and fruitful. Of course, loving therapy, proper medication, creative expression, and loving relationships have helped. But it is primarily my Christian faith that has enabled me to prosper. I am now able to grow, find meaning, and enjoy life.

Before becoming "saved," I searched for "religion" through searing pain. When I heard about Christianity, I grabbed the nail–pierced hand in faith, and Jesus Christ didn't let go of me! It is the best thing that has ever happened to me.

How to Teach a Schizophrenic

Schizophrenics deserve dignity and respect. Unlike a physical disability, schizophrenia is sad because it's almost as if each patient speaks his or her private language. While a remedy for a physical ailment can be applied generally to all, when it comes to schizophrenia one type of therapy might work in some but not all. For a therapist to be effective, he has to have an ear to hear. To untangle a patient's woven web it takes time, patience, and (I have found) a therapist who is himself a Christian.

A therapist should be a guide who can lead the patient through a new life with faith, transitional or not, that works for the particular patient. A therapist who is a strong humanitarian is a must. Unless the patient discovers Christianity, the search for peace could be long and the situation quite terminal. I know that without this key, Christianity, I could not have survived. Personal growth can be slow, and the terrain rough. This is why a therapist who can provide the proper spiritual reference point is essential. The world view (as opposed to the Christian life of the spirit) is a toxin which can destroy love even before it is born in the heart. Christianity, I feel, is the most loving religion of all, and can be accessed through any door. No one is barred. Schizophrenics require love like anyone else, and possibly more so.

Other religions, such as those which involve reincarnation, may view schizophrenia as a punishment for a sinful previous existence. The schizophrenic patient is not the living embodiment of sin, and he or she can find spiritual fulfillment on earth, provided that Jesus Christ is the key. Through Christ the many sins, depressions, fears, terrors, and sicknesses can be dealt with. Spiritual peace can be found.

What the Schizophrenic Experience Has Been Like

Even though I was saved, recovery from schizophrenia took quite a while. I tried to avoid stressful situations and get as much rest as possible. I performed ego–boosting—not to feel superior to others—but to help me cope with my new world view. I mean, I considered myself " religious" before I was saved, so I needed some time to digest this new and potent wine known as Christianity. I must admit that, prior to my salvation, religion frightened me. I associated " religion" (even though I was drawn to it) with the frightening, out–of control, abusive side of human nature. I felt as if God were a mystery that could not be understood by anyone at any time, and that it was mere madness to suggest otherwise. When I opened up to the light I did it piecemeal, a little at a time, not unlike the way a flower opens to the sun. I eased myself away from the world view, though for a while I needed reassurance from others. I was not quite ready to accept reassurance merely from God. The tag " born again" frightened me because it seemed too over the edge, too " religious." I needed time to reinforce my faith before I could cross over entirely into my new life. In this stage of my life I was a child in the womb, waiting to be born. The seed had been implanted and I was already alive in the faith, but I had not as yet reached my fulfillment.

As Christians we teeter back and forth between the world and our Christianity. I compare it to the effect that you get when you come back out into the light after having been in a dark movie theater. We become accustomed to the dark, somewhat like the way we become accustomed to the world upon exposure to it. Once we leave the theater, it takes time for our eyes to adjust. I confess that I am sometimes taken in by world views. I strive for discipline, and as I walk in the light I am getting better at resisting temptation. I am becoming refined, like gold made in Christ's image. I methodically abandon the sins that I have conquered and attempt to overcome the finer, more subtle offenses to God.

For my first ten years as a believer I have tried as much as possible to make my faith in Jesus Christ paramount. For it is the template upon which everything is molded, and it is the axis upon which everything revolves. I have learned to love self discipline, as well as self analysis, and therapy, because each of these things involve Christ. I think upon nothing except how I can grow in my faith and help others. Witnessing to others about my belief has had great dividends.

It helps others, and it helps me. I have done a great deal of this for the last ten years, and it has contributed greatly to my growth. I witness verbally or through tracts everywhere I go. My recovery is, of course, in and of itself a strong Christian testimony.

I try to allow myself a healthy amount of " fun time." That is, I try not to stress myself out by having to do everything " right this second." I try not to feel forced or pressured. I have forever abol-

ished from my life the " Rushin' flu!" I love myself. I am a tem
God. The Holy Spirit resides in me.

Of course, anyone with schizophrenia should avoid alco....
beverages, and certainly no one should dabble with recreational drugs.

Because I experience quite a bit of ahedonia, I do drink coffee
in moderation. Too much coffee wires my nerves, thereby poisoning
my mind with psychoses. When I've had too much coffee, I don't
think clearly. I usually drink coffee in coordination with a specific
activity. In a moderate dose, coffee enables me to enjoy an activity. I
have to be careful, however, to use coffee only when doing a recreational activity. It's really a bad idea for me to drink coffee when I'm
doing something serious (e.g. writing a business letter). For me that
would be tantamount to mixing business with pleasure. Pleasure is
good in and of itself, but it does not belong in the boardroom.

Activities that I like to combine with coffee include going for
drives, hiking in a natural area, swimming, painting, talking wrth
friends, thinking, looking at art, and listening to music.

Thinking, Discipline

I try to avoid negative thinking and carnal appetites. That is, I
try not to focus on anything too worldly or loathsome. If I see an
animal carcass on the side of the road I try to redirect my thoughts so
as not to become obsessed with the horror. When I get a negative
thought I analyze it, reject it, and replace it with a positive Christian
thought. I try to meditate upon things that are noble, good, just, lovely,
pure. Because it is difficult for me to read, I devote my quiet time to
Christian growth. I apply the Bible, either through witnessing, or doing
good. I do judge my spiritual growth at least once a week so that I can
see what needs to be confessed, what I can do for others and for God.
I examine the mistakes I've made. I try to learn from them and to
keep myself from repeating them. I consider changes to be made in
my thinking pattern and what I should be doing now in my walk with
the Lord. Am I reading the Bible every day? Am I setting a good
example to others? Am I attending church regularly? Have I been

confessing all my sins? Have I been analyzing my walk and rewarding myself for good behavior? Have I been witnessing to others?

I realize that sometimes God guides me in ways that I don't understand and that sometimes when I am walking fruitfully with God he will prune my life in order to make it even more fruitful. For me the utmost is to become more like his Son. I try to understand that I will not understand entirely or have everything spelled out for me, but I know at least that it is good to except the good with the bad. A rose is beautiful but full of thorns. I know that through acceptance of my affliction I can grow as a Christian. Acceptance certainly has been more useful to me than complaining or feeling sorry for myself. I can learn from my circumstance and stretch, not shrink.

I will not look back at the past. I will not becomeobsessed with bad things. I am grateful for the good things that God has so graciously given me, especially the gift of my salvation. The fact that I am saved inspires me to go out there and give to others. I call these my love minutes. I appreciate the things of the spirit that I already have, including my salvation, and I anticipate the many spiritual gifts to come. If someone in the past has offended or mistreated me, I forgive. The offense is in the past, and the past does not concern me. I don't keep a checklist of all the wrongs that others have done to me (this is God's concern, not mine). What concerns me is my salvation and serving God in the present. I am like a fruit, ripening, slowly burgeoning, or like a flower opening slowly in the early light.

Time is important to me, because that is how we measure a life. When will someone die? We cannot know, because that's God's business. Our job is to help others while we can. We mustn't be tardy. In fact, it is already very late.

I forgive myself. I love myself. By loving myself I can help others, and grow.

I avoid abusive people and situations that will weaken me spiritually. I am a temple of God. I love God and I love myself.

I try not to compete with others. I accept my inadequacies and emphasize my good points. I value and judge myself on how good a person I am in God's eyes. He has redeemed me as His child and I am now acceptable to Him. I obtain my self–validation based on how God sees me, not in an ephemeral, ever–changing way that man sees me, in the world–view. The world view judges you based on your personal appearance or how big your bank account is. It judges you according to your occupation, your talent, or your brain power. None of these things can last, and if they are used to do harm by a heart that has an evil intent, they can destroy. Schizophrenia is difficult to deal with without the added constriction of these things. These things don't last but merely pass away. I fix my eyes on the unseen. I emphasize the spiritual and the good, as defined by the Bible.

I number my days and plan in a practical way, but ultimately I place the whole thing in God's hands. By putting His will first, I relieve myself of a great burden. I know that God is good because I have seen the evidence in my own life. If God weren't good, I wouldn't be able to throw off my mental shackles. But He is, and I have, praise the Lord! I can't go wrong if I put God at the controls. I feel more comfortable, and even more so if I am not sinning actively. If I try to take control of my life through active rebellion or sin, then I am on dangerous ground.

Anger

I become angry on occasion. Anger can catch fire and spread. I try to avoid anger, or channel it into a constructive activity, such as painting.

Prayer

On my knees or quietly in my mind I offer up all of my thoughts and decisions to God in humble prayer. I lay my petitions and re-quests before God and know that He hears my prayers. I also know that he does not always answer them the way I understand. This is His will, and we can get somewhat of an indication of His will by reading the Bible. Whatever happens to me in this life, I will benefit, because everything turns out for the good for those who love God.

Prayer is great for peace. It sustains, giving me nourishment in a barren wilderness. And seeing a prayer answered can be a very fulfilling experience. An answered prayer can provide me comfort. It reassures me that the God who helped me once can help me many times over.

Dealing with My Past

I realize that a lot of the miseries that I experienced prior to my salvation in Christ were due to the fact that I was not yet " acceptable" in God's eyes. He was in the right to punish my sin, and I suffered the consequences of His wrath. This wrath was absorbed by Jesus Christ on the cross. When I accepted Christ, I was made righteous in God's eyes and entered into a relationship with Him as His child. I cannot blame God for any of my past misery, for He is holy, just, omnipotent, omniscient, and omnipresent. He created me. He knows me intimately, He knows my frame. It says in the Bible that once you are saved, God will never give you more than you can handle. This is one of the most beautiful of Biblical truths!

How the Fundamentals of My Born–Again Experience Have Helped Me

The " good news" of the Gospel has provided me with a real working force in my life. At long last my life is in control and I am a functioning human being!

First, I received Jesus Christ as my personal Savior in my heart, according to how the Bible specifies. I humbled myself as a child. Then I immersed myself in the " word," the Bible and what the Bible specifies for Christian growth. I also relied on my Christian therapist. My therapist in effect became my sounding board, and he enabled me to test the validity of the Christian experience. I mean, I wanted to be sure that my newfound faith was not just another psychotic episode. My therapist was instrumental in grounding me in the real world, where I could see the truths of the Bible revealed daily in my life. Each time I saw something Biblical work for me or come true, I would test it with my therapy. I questioned the soundness of my mental health. I also relied on the Christian media (e.g. bookstores, Christian talk stations), as well as the clergy. If I were psychotic, then certainly it seemed like I had a lot of company!

Regardless of whether I understood the purpose for a particular thing, I believed that God is good and that the Bible is the infallible word of God. If something went wrong in my life, I accepted this as being important in God's larger scheme for the universe. And so I kept applying to see if there was validity to the Christian experience. I tested like a scientist, but I also approached my Christianity as a child. And I don't mean merely in the way that I accepted Him as my personal Savior, but also in how I " walked" with him on a daily basis. God is good. It all begins with that. If you're a schizophrenic, you've got to hold onto that fact. It's a prerequisite.

Believing in God's ultimate goodness allowed me to reach the point where I could no longer deny His existence, nor His very real presence in my life. I kept growing and testing and confirming till after ten years of being a believer I reached the point where I had assurance of my salvation. The Christian experience works for me. It is sane, non–chaotic, anything but reckless, orderly, honest, and genuine.

Basically there are three principles that I need to know and fluidly apply in my Christian walk. They are, first of all, the supposition that God is good, and that the Bible—and not my flavor–of the–day emotions—is the gauge to measure reality. And, thirdly, that there are no coincidences in the life of a believer. This last principle may sound a bit psychotic to the unbeliever, but I assure the reader that I've tested this through years of proper medication, sound therapy, loving relationships, and creative expression. God working through me has enabled me to accept myself while at the same time accepting God as the utmost. Fulfilled Biblical promises (e.g. such as the promise to heal the believer) are essential because they enable the Christian to help others. They also glorify God, and can inspire the unbeliever to take that decisive lurch away from the shade and toward the light.. What can be a stronger witness than the Bible coming alive and working as a template in my life!

God is Good

While reading the Bible, questions commonly surface in my mind. This can be frustrating, because quite often I refer to the Bible to find answers for questions. Instead of my initial concern, I'll wind up with three or four things I'll want to go over with my pastor. I think to myself, man, if this is how it is for the believer, imagine how confusing the Bible must be to the unenlightened! Why, therefore, does God blind the eyes of the unbeliever? If God is good, there must be a reason in the larger scheme of things beyond the smoke and mirrors, right? But, of course, the human intellect is limited. We don't understand. God is bigger. This is why we need to see beyond our selfish motives. It is far better to serve God than to compromise our spirit–led lives with the human ego. By putting God's will first we help others. On a personal level, I have found that trusting God perpetuates an orderly and harmonic Christian life, and where there is peace in life there is growth, or—if the reader will excuse the term— evolution.

God created everything. It is His plan. He knows what He is doing. We don't have a right to tell Him what to do. Why rebel? We should just try to help others and allow them the chance to be " saved" through our witness and example. Christianity is a beautiful thing. A true Christian does not condemn other religions. Christianity is not a religion of negation, but of affirmation.

We are not nay–sayers. We don't belittle people's beliefs, but share with them the truth as we believe and don't compromise. We want to share with others the " good news" we have found not out of religious bigotry, but because we love them and want to offer them the gift of Christian salvation. We should not use the Bible to glorify ourselves, nor should we use it to prop up our selfish motives. Christianity is not about ethnic intimidation, and a genuine

Christian witness does not " beat over the head." If anything, this kind of witness over the years, has kept more people away than it has saved. As the hymn goes, " they will know we are Christians by our love," and not necessarily by our political action committees, nor by the various religious bigots (they know who they are) who masquerade as Christians.

God is Reality

Would Christianity work for you? If you think it might, and you'd like to take the first step out of the darkness and see whether the Christian life might work for you, I recommend that you refer to the Bible. Study it, consult pastors, and compare texts. Most importantly, visit a Biblically sound church. Non–Biblical speculation about Christ might be helpful to the learned theologian schooled on Hebrew and Greek, but as for the everyday Christian nothing is better than the solid bedrock of the Biblical truth. Even more so if the believer is a schizophrenic, since nothing can be more invaluable to this sort of person than a place to ground his or her spiritual life. On days when I feel isolated and out of touch with reality, I can turn to the pages of Isaiah, or Job, or the gospel of Mark, and immediately be subjected to a reality check. God is greater than any delusion, than any insidious bout with depression.

Because of my firm conviction that the Christian faith will work for any person, I urge the unbeliever to try it for a little while and test whether or not it offers any benefit to his or her life. I'm guessing that it will, and I almost feel like wanting to go on cable–television so that I could urge viewers to accept Christianity with a money–back guarantee (if it doesn't work after 30 days)! But receiving Jesus like a child (as the Bible says), and walking with Christ as a child, is crucial. Accepting what the Bible says without question (the Bible being the infallible word of God), allows you to see whether or not it can work for you. If you don't consider the way of the cross and apply the Bible's principles, you're not giving Christianity a fair chance. If you let your emotions be your spiritual guides, you are relying on things which change on a daily basis. You run the risk of turning psychotic, and losing all connection with reality. If you are a believing Christian, irrational states can derail you like a railroad spur leading to a field of tall grass. If you want to be grounded in reality, trust the Bible, and stay on track. Trusting in emotions can seriously damage your walk with Christ, and although you are held by Christ and cannot lose your salvation, you can transform the Christian experience from a positive into a negative one.

It is best if the believer does not seek out emotions. Emotions tend to put the self on a pedestal, instead of God.

There Are No Coincidences with God

The Bible stresses that nothing on this earth is coincidental. This concept can be difficult for the schizophrenic patient to grasp, however, since everything to him can seem coincidental.

To the schizophrenic patient, for example, even two people talking nonchalantly on a street corner about the weather can have personal, usually sinister significance. The trick is for the patient to stay focused on God, and to not get too preoccupied with the self. Two people talking about the weather are not about you or I, but about how God manifests Himself in the seemingly insignificant. Overhearing a conversation about the " hot spell we've been having" or about killer tornadoes in Texas can remind me that the God who made creation is still on the throne and that there is nothing so defenseless as a man in this world without faith. Human life is so fragile that even a gust of wind can undermine it, but not so the soul that is saved in Christ. Armed with the armor of God the schizophrenic patient who is afraid of public exposure can go wherever he or she pleases, because everything, even an apathetic hello or a frenzied wave, relates to God (and not to the patient).

Though I refrain from being preoccupied with material things, I do sometimes use them to further my walk. Whenever I do something good, such as witness to another about Christ, I allow myself to enjoy something material. This is called positive reinforcement, and it helps my mental state as much as my spiritual walk. Too often people who grew up in a Christian church were led to formulate the wrong opinion about Christianity, that it was a harsh religion of brutal punishments. A friend of mine who grew up in the Catholic faith struggled for years before he accepted Christianity because of a fourth grade nun who crudely attempted to terrorize her students into belief. She didn't reward for good behavior, but merely punished for suspected faults, castigating her charges for being " dirty, filthy things, unworthy of God." Too often in life the setting we are in revolves around negative reinforcement. In the military, in our place of employment, we are more often than not punished for the bad that we do, and neglected for the good. In psychiatry some therapists utilize exercises like "flooding" in order to flush out painful, negative experiences. It's a shame that there's not enough emphasis on reliving joyful moments, like a scenic car ride in the snow. Christianity is not about subjecting the believer to insufferabletrials. I repeat: God never gives the believer more than he can handle.

I don't avoid material things because I believe that God created the world so that we could enjoy life. When He created the universe, he saw that it was good, not an evil monstrosity. Only Satan would want us to beat ourselves over the head and retract into our shell. When we don't allow ourselves an innocent pleasure here and there we allow the serpent to gain a foothold in our belief system. We might even lose sight of the good and begin confusing God with Satan.

This may cause us even to rebel and sin. I am reminded of the generic fire and brimstone radio preacher who may become so obsessed with the devil's stranglehold over the flesh, that he may after a while seem like the devil's mouthpiece, boasting about the serpent's presence, for example, in even the most innocuous of children's TV shows. Certainly there are elements of theworld at war with the spirit, but I assure the reader that there is far more evidence of God working in the universe than there is of the serpent!

God is love, but Satan has been trying to convince Christians that God doesn't love them. It worked with Adam and Eve, and

Satan has been succeeding ever since. Material things are to be enjoyed. It is after all the intent of the heart that matters most. This is what God looks at. The enjoyment of a material thing can allow you some " space" before your next disciplinary leap. Sports teams whose ultimate goal is winning the championship may celebrate beating a quarterfinal opponent. The Christian who enjoys a peaceful moment is like the surging sports team, even if there really is no end in this life to the championship drive.

The pleasure derived from a material thing is good, so long as it is not an excuse for doing God's will. For this reason it is good not to be too obsessed with material things. Christians who are overly concerned with acquiring expensive cars or forty–room mansions can provide a bad witness. Such a believer is sometimes easily used by a consumer culture that stresses buy, buy, buy.

Rewards

The Bible refers to rewards in heaven. This is not, however, like giving candy to a baby. Christ states in the Bible that seeking these rewards is important. Of course, we should not seek solely a personal reward, since our number one motivation ought to be love for God and doing His will. Keeping our eye on rewards in heaven can be helpful in that it gives us a purpose, and furthers our growth. It might also attract unbelievers who might be fearful of dying. The prospect of an eternity spent basking in the glow of Christ's affection might also help us through a rough day, or an illness. By sometimes reminding ourselves of the rewards in the great beyond, we strengthen our faith and further our spiritual evolution. Most importantly, the promise of an eternal life in heaven beyond the boundaries of flesh and time glorifies God. What a loving religion, that offers rewards as an understandable context for growth!

Straight Lines

In your spiritual walk, be "all out for Christ." I've found that this will enhance your having assurance of salvation, and that you won't want to drift. If you start to drift, it is sometimes hard to get back on course and the evil might try to upset you. And if you are newly saved or experiencing psychoses, drifting can be very dangerous. It can generate doubts and fears about God, which are unfounded. The new recruit is especially at risk, since he may not know enough about the facts found in scripture. Satan might then use this as an opportunity to lure you from worshiping and serving God, which should be the Christian's prime concern. Satan wants you to disobey God, and will try to achieve this objective anyway that he can. So, it's best to do as the Bible recommends for growth. Biblical knowledge is a must! The more you know and apply, the better off you will be.

Read your Bible. Meditate on the word, and most importantly apply what you've read. Go to church. Have a fellowship with believers. Confess your sins, because this wipes the record of your sins clean, and they won't be brought up again. This permits you to travel on the smooth straight and narrow.

Witnessing is a quick and easy way to having an intimate relationship with God. Witnessing is commanded. What could be more rewarding than God using you to win others to Christ? A soul is a life, and what upright man or woman would let a fellow human being go without warning into perdition? Witnessing involves interaction, which is contact with a fellow traveler in this universe. There is no better way to see God at work in the world. How great it will be to meet in heaven those whom we have won to Christ! We pass by millions in our life: that old man with the cane, in the wheel chair, using the voice box. These people could be changed forever by a brief sentence or a chosen word.

I don't do what I do as a Christian by rote, or because I am ritually required to (e.g. such as confess my sins). I do what I do because I have learned to love God, and I am what I am because of this personal, non–terrestrial relationship. So, I enjoy serving Him. I see when He rewards my good behavior and I know when I have done something wrong, because He chastens me. This is never done in a cruel or reckless way, but only to guide me gently in the right paths because he cares about me. There is no coincidence to anything in my life. If I experience failure, I consider it a " successful failure," because it helps me understand God's will for my life. It allows me to confess my sins, and thereby get closer to God. I am not too concerned with being perfect. I just want God to be my friend.

The saints in the Bible were human and had their faults also. God accepts human frailty, because as Christians sin enables us to learn and grow. We are perpetually remaking ourselves in the likeness of Jesus Christ, until that day in heaven when we will attain perfect conformity to Him. I praise the Lord for my faults, because it draws me closer to Him and helps others become saved. I am not Miss Perfect. Miss Forgiven is more like it. I believe that this outlook is healthy and reasonable. If people see that you are not perfect, this allows them a choice to become a believer. If it works for her, it can work for me. By saying that there is no good in someone else's non–Christian growth or religion, or spiritual belief system, I can jeopardize a witness. There is ample evidence that any creed can nurture the wounded psyche. But only one is genuine, only one can rescue the soul. We must allow the non–believer room to search and find God. It makes sense to treat someone the way you would want to be treated. Seeking man can find God.

God has been kind, compassionate, and patient like a father. Before I was saved, I wallowed in the ignorance of mistaken notions. To paraphrase Isaiah, though I had eyes, I could not see. I thought that God was cruel. But this is not God. God is good. He has good personality traits, as defined by the Bible. You have to cross over from death to life, from being a non–believer to a believer to see. Spiritual deafness must be purged, and the one way to do this is through receiving Jesus Christ. Once you have received you must read the Bible, though it is more important to apply what you've learned and to grow. Those suffering from spiritual deafness may read the Bible and appreciate it for its poetry and reliable history, but the message of the cross and the truths of the Bible are as unintelligible to them as an infant's gibberish. This is why there are a lot of misconceptions about the Bible and why some doubt that God is good. People who are not saved just don't get it.

I used to think that God was cruel and enjoyed hurting and killing people. He doesn't take pleasure in the death of anyone. This is why there is a way out, a way to a new life and eternal life: Jesus Christ. Satan gets us to believe that God is not good. God has a certain personality and made things a certain way. God is holy, and we have to be made right in His eyes. We as fleshly human beings are all sinners. No one is good enough by himself to get to heaven. No amount of good works can help a man attain paradise. The only ticket to the great eternal show in the sky is through faith in Jesus Christ. We must believe that He came down to earth in human form and absorbed the wrath of God for our sins. We must believe that it is through Christ's agony on the cross that we are made acceptable in God's eyes. Once saved, we no longer offend Him. Christ comes into our lives, our sins are forgiven, and we become children of God. We receive eternal life and begin the great adventure that God created us to experience.

God's Sovereignty and Our Free Will

I used to think before I was saved that God made everything turn out so horribly. I now believe that though God is sovereign, he gives humans the free will to sin. He does this (and this is not fully explained in the Bible) because sin acts as a catalyst for confession and forgiveness. Sin is therefore comparable to the devil in Goethe's Faust, who constantly sets evil in motion only to have it in the end generating good. I don't blame God for the evil that happens. He merely wound up the universe and let it go.

Evolution

From Genesis to the gospels there is a steady progression in the Bible. It almost seems as if the situation gradually gets better for the believer. We begin with the faith of Abraham, and this progresses to the almost superhuman faith of Job. At this point mankind becomes capable of receiving the Messiah, and hence the prophetic works emphasizing Christ's descent to earth emerge. Finally Christ walks among us, the gates of death are opened, and the Holy Spirit comes to dwell in humankind. But it isn't over yet. We as Christians continue to improve. The Holy Spirit is still among us, and there is the promise of the ultimate return of Christ and the thousand–year reign. This is in and of itself an indication of order, an indication that God is good. It makes sense to me that there would be a spiritual afterlife, and goodness. Heaven—what a concept. I cling to that.

Resources on the Web

an afterword by the editor
J. Rankin, RN, MSN
Clinical Nurse Specialist, Neurosciences

The Internet today provides some of the fastest access to information sources, and support groups. Indeed, the major problem one faces, if computer literate, is that of sorting through the sheer mass of information available, as well as that of discerning which support groups or network meet one's needs.

Simply as an experiment, go to any of the search engines on your internet browser, and type in the word, "schizophrenia." Even if one were to do no further searches, that alone would bring up some of the most detailed lists of online resources one could desire.

However, before going into a long search for information or networking opportunities, it is probably best to determine what your own goals may be. "Nosce te ipsum," said the Latin, echoing the ancient Greek oracle of Apollo at Delphi, "gnothi seauton," *Know Thyself*. For, knowing what your needs and goals are, is the first and best step for any journey along the so–called "Information Highway."

No matter how simply stated, even if it is only one stated goal, you are way ahead of the game, once you have formulated it as the beginning of your search; for, it is literally the beginning of your entire journey.

For example, what is it you really need? Often, if not most

often, people facing a health crisis, or an illness, will seek information on the disease or problem itself. And, maybe they need that. But, often as not, the real need is not to know about the disease in detail, but how to cope with it. How to find the human and spiritual resources to face what has to be faced, and come to terms with the meaning it has for one's life.

Simply put, one has to determine how the thing is going to be approached, and how one hopes (or plans) to emerge on the other side of it. At that point, the need is not simply for information about the problem itself, but about how other people have dealt with it, and who might be out there, for support, for networking, and for counsel and encouragement. That's a different search.

We all need to be "in charge" of our own health care, and to set the terms on which we will accept or refuse care, or what care we seek. But, that does not mean becoming more of an expert in the problem than the doctor, for example. Or the nurse. Or any professional who may help you, or whose counsel you may seek. That may happen, but it is always limited in range and focus. More often, the need of the person undergoing the process is for a way to respond, not a need to establish and direct one's own therapy. Again, that's a "horse of a different color," a different search.

Most of all, it is important to recall that the person suffering (undergoing) a disease or illness, or such process is a *patient* in that exact and original meaning of the term: to undergo, to suffer, if one looks to the Latin roots of our tongue. The immediate references are religious: the Passion (Suffering) of Christ; the Nicene Creed's statement that Christ suffered and was buried (passus et sepultus est). But the point of all that is to look at the simple fact that people often —always?—experience two things: the disease, and their suffering. It is almost as though they are two separate things, sometimes; and that they can only be resolved by re–integrating the shattered and dis–integrated personality of the person undergoing the process (the patient). (No one who really understands the issues ever refers to a patient as a "client.") It is telling that in Scripture, the concept of "righteousness" is one of wholeness, of integration of the whole person, which can also be expressed as "godliness." Hence, for Jews, as for many of our parents in the Faith, this unity of "body, mind, and spirit," was expressed as "the Heart." And when the Prophet says: "Let justice roll down like the waters, and righteousness roll on like a mighty stream," he is referring to what happens when the shattered person acquires integrity, wholeness—or what happens when that becomes the standard mode of a whole society.

And again, if one's needs or goals lie here, then this is again another search.

Step One: Decide what your needs are, or seek out others with whom you can talk, to determine what needs really are, and how they can be clearly stated. Stay simple. Just one clearly stated need will do. But, as many as are necessary.

Step Two: When? What is the time frame in which your need—your one need, or each given need you are able to define— must be addressed? Not necessarily met, but at least addressed.

Step Three: What is the desired outcome, or goal, for each need determined.

Step Four: What must one do—now, later, whenever. But, at least one goal should address the first need, the first goal in the here and now.

Here and Now. Hegel's old "hic et nunc." Doesn't matter what you're saying, doesn't matter what you're doing—if it is not focused in the realities of the here and now, you're beating the bushes in vain.

So, having taken these steps, WHAT?

Well, how about something simple, like: "OK, now what do I need to know or find out, to meet this goal, and do what I must do?"

Hey! I'm glad you asked!

Go to the Internet, and start your search engines!

Making it Simpler

What I'd recommend most, after a quick bit of fun just getting acquainted with the Net, is to focus on one or two primary resources, that are useful to just about everybody. From there, you can branch out, and eventually you will find that there are more things out there than you can look at in a lifetime.

For now, let's look at one primary resource: the National Library of Medicine, and AHCPR, which can be accessed there.

The National Library of Medicine, or NLM, can introduce you to not only the professional literature on a disease, but also can help you find material for other kinds of searches, too: support groups, self–help, and so on.

You don't really need to know the Internet address at first: just go to search, and write in the search pattern box: "National Library of Medicine." (The quotes mean the search engine is to use the exact words or phrase, as a unit. Otherwise, the engine would use each word as a keyword, which can give you some strange connections.)

When you have done this, and have identified which sites you are going to visit, record the Internet addresses of the NLM, or AHCPR, or any site you visit (their "URL," which appears at the top of your web browser, so you always know where you are).

Grateful Med
When you develop a little experience, you can begin to conduct searches of the huge NLM databases of books, articles, and such,

using their popular search engine, *The Grateful Med.* It is online, and it is free—and it was pretty costly not many years back.

It will take a bit to learn how to use keywords and the NLM's "MESH" headings to get information, but the work is quite rewarding. One can locate books, videos, articles, and the like, very rapidly, and download short descriptions of each, or print them online.

Type the word, "schizophrenia," for example, as a simple search. A lot of books and articles. Too many. So, you can combine words(schizophrenia and teenagers) or separate terms, to sharpen the focus.

But, you will learn all this.

Next, I'd recommend the Library of Congress, which by law must receive two copies of all books published in the United States, and which aids publishers in cataloging their publications. Almost every book cataloged by the Library of Congress (LC) will have an LC card number, which helps immensely in locating publications.

Find the LC by using your search engine the first time, just as you did with the National Library of Medicine. You will note that both agencies, being official ones, have URLs that end in ".gov," which means (obviously) "government," as opposed to ".com," which means "commercial," or ".org," which refers to an organization, which can be public, non–profit, membership, or whatever. In the future, there may be many other endings of URLs, but for now, with InterNIC the only licensing agency, these three endings predominate.

Now, Let's Get a Little More Specific

Calling upon the American Psychiatric Association, or the American Psychological Association, the American Medical Association, the American Nurses Association, and so on, will become very easy, as you acquire the necessary Internet skills. And they will provide a great deal of help and information.

You don't need a lot of guidance for that. Just do it.

However, let's point out a couple of initial websites that might be very useful. Once there, you will be able to branch out to a number of other sites, to find either the information you may need, or support groups.

http://schizophrenia.mentalhelp.net/

Whose heading is: "All About Schizophrenia — Mental Health Net."

Right at the top, you will find a link button to drkoop.com, the practice website of the former Surgeon General, Dr. Koop. This site has taken off this year, and had a successful IPO offering on Wall Street, which helped finance it better.

We recommend, first, that you begin on Mental Health Net with the book, *Your Complete **Well–Connected** Guide to Schizophrenia*, which located on the first page, just under Dr. Koop's link.

The *Guide* discusses symptoms, treatment, online resources, organizations, online support, and research information for persons who have to deal with schizophrenia. Excerpts fill the first screen of the site: "What is it?" "You are not to blame." "So what causes it?" and "What do I do now?" are some of the topics discussed very clearly and directly.

http://members.aol.com/leonardjk/USA.htm

This URL supplies a list of U. S. Support Organizations, state by state, and where possible, locality by locality. The list consists primarily of state and local associates of the National Alliance for the Mentally Ill (NAMI). Often, there is only one associate in a state, but there are many with websites of their own. Addresses, phone numbers, contact names, meeting times are provided.

No general recommendation can be given for NAMI or any of its affiliates—nor, for that matter, any of the URLs one may stumble across. Nor, am I suggesting one should depart competent care to cast oneself adrift on the Net. Heaven Forbid! Rather, here are some possible starting places for information–seeking, and support. However, the best support, if one can get it, is much closer to home: the people who know and love you, from family and friends, to your professional consultants, and the community.

Nevertheless, if one needs it, the Web is a fine place to seek information, and to network. We've not even touched the surface, for their are "Lists" (email discussion groups) and "ChatRooms" (live, online email exhanges at set hours), and many other opportunities.

May this orientation to the Web benefit you, and at least put you in a place where—as an old cowboy friend of my Dad used to say—"I'm commencin' to begin to start."

God bless.

In this journey, as in any other, the issue is to get up and get into motion. The story is told of a man, long ago, who was told by the messenger of the gods, that to obtain salvation, he had to walk one million times around the great circle of the globe. This task, to walk a million times around the earth, so overwhelmed his imagination, that he sat down—almost fell down—on the ground, and began to think about it.

For ten thousand years, he sat there, and pondered it.

Then, one day—he got up, and began walking.

In Christ's love,
    J. Rankin, at Roseville, 11/30/99 (Feast of Saint Andrew).